Healing with You

A CHRISTMAS ROMANCE

LOVE IN HARMONY BOOK ONE
KALAYNA MARIE

Copyright © 2024 Kalayna Marie
www.authorkalaynamarie.com

All rights reserved.
The characters and events portrayed in this book are fictitious. Any similarity to real persons, living or dead, is coincidental and not intended by the author.

No part of this book may be reproduced, or stored in a retrieval system, or transmitted in any form or by any means, electronic, mechanical, photocopying, recording, or otherwise, without express written permission of the publisher.

Cover Design and Formatting by Kalayna Marie

Edited by Alexa Thomas | The Fiction Fix
www.thefictionfix.com

Proofread by Tori Lewis

ISBN: 979-8-9918691-0-2
Imprint: Independently published

*for those who are grieving:
may you find your peace and healing*

CONTENT WARNING

Please note:
This book contains sensitive subject matter that may be triggering to some readers. It is my hope that I've handled these subjects delicately and respectfully in the process of bringing these characters their happily ever after

For a detailed list of trigger warnings, please visit
www.authorkalaynamarie.com

PLAYLIST

listen on spotify

Mr. Perfectly Fine—Taylor Swift
Walked Through Hell—Anson Seabra
Silent Night—Bing Crosby
Shout Out to My Ex—Little Mix
Please Come Home for Christmas—Eagles
Christmas Tree Farm—Taylor Swift
Start of Something Good—Daughtry
I GUESS I'M IN LOVE—Clinton Kane
Chances—Five For Fighting
Fallin' for You—Colbie Caillat
Everything has Changed—Taylor Swift, Ed Sheeran
IF YOU GO DOWN (I'M GOING DOWN TOO)—Kelsea Ballerini
Better Together—Luke Combs
Say Don't Go—Taylor Swift
Afterglow—Taylor Swift
If December Never Ends—Anson Seabra
Before You—Benson Boone
You Are in Love—Taylor Swift
Carry You Home—Alex Warren
Hometown Christmas—NEEDTOBREATHE
Winter Dreams (Brandon's Song)—Kelly Clarkson

CHAPTER ONE
JANA

The Louisiana humidity soaks through my sundress, leaving me sweaty and uncomfortable. I try to adjust the straps, hoping to relieve the discomfort, but it only makes things worse. Glancing around the office, I push myself into a standing position. Nobody seems to notice me, too busy with their phone calls and solitaire games to care.

I leave my cubicle, irritated at how my thighs chafe with every step I take. The bathroom is empty when I get there, and I'm grateful for it. I gather a wad of paper towels and run them under cold water before heading to a stall.

Dabbing the cool towels over my neck, I fish my phone from my pocket and dial.

"Jay, why the hell are you calling me at eight in the morning?" my best friend asks, her voice cracking.

"It's nine here, and I didn't think about it," I reply, moving the damp paper towels over my heated skin. "It's already 78 degrees here, and I'm soaking wet from the humidity."

"You're the one who decided to go live in Satan's buttcrack," she says grumpily. The sound of rustling fabric fills the space between us, and her voice is slightly muffled when she speaks again. "I'm assuming you're not just calling to complain about the weather."

I sigh, studying the metal door in front of me like it holds the answers to life's questions. She's right, of course. She always is, always has been.

"I just don't know why I'm still here," I say softly.

"Me neither, Jay." Hadlee Scott has never been one to beat around the bush, especially not when she's exhausted. "You only moved out there to be with George, and you're not with him anymore—you're not, are you?"

"No." I shake my head vehemently, knocking some curls free from the loose bun I'd thrown them in this morning. "No, I'm done with him. He officially moved out a couple weeks ago."

"*Good.*" I can picture her relaxing back into her pillows, a satisfied smile pulling at her delicate features. "I never did like that asshole."

"It's actually *not* good," I say, ignoring her jab at my taste in men. Lifting my free hand to my mouth, I bite at the cuticle of my thumb.

"What do you mean? Of course it is."

"No," I sigh, my hand dropping to my lap. This breakup had come as no surprise to anyone...except me. Maybe it was my unabashed love for love that kept me from seeing it, but I was always the last to recognize the toxicity in my relationships. The breakup was a long time coming, even if I didn't want to acknowledge it. "I'm not talking about the breakup—we were splitting the rent, and now, it's all on me."

"Oh."

"I can't afford that apartment on my lousy pay." Tears spring to my eyes, and I shake my head with a sharp laugh. My heart is breaking for a whole other reason at this point.

"Then break your lease and move back home," Hadlee says. *Home?* I stay silent, my heart in my throat. "You can stay in my spare room until you find something more permanent."

Moving back to Harmony feels impossible. It's been a lifetime since I left, and the memories that come with it could easily drown me. "I don't know if I can do that, Lee."

"I know it's been a while," she says, "but you know you've always been welcome here."

"I know," I say. And I do. But it hasn't felt like home in a long time—not since my parents died. I've been searching for that unmistakable feeling of home ever since, to no avail. My chest aches as sadness washes over me. "I just don't know if I can. I haven't been back since the funeral."

"I know, sweetie." Her voice is low, and I know she's feeling the same melancholy. Hadlee grew up in the house down the street, and our parents had been best friends since college. She practically lived at our house during her parents' nasty divorce, so losing my mom and dad had been just as hard on her as it was on me. They were her second family. "Don't you think it's time, though? It's been six years."

I stay quiet, my heart beating roughly against my ribcage. Harmony holds so many fond memories, yet they're all tainted by loss. But maybe Hadlee's right. Maybe it's time to release the grief and pain associated with the small town and return to Harmony.

I toss the damp paper towel into the trash before running a hand down my face. "I'll think about it."

"That's all I'm asking," she says with a yawn. "I've got the guest room all made up for you, so you just need to say the word."

Warmth fills my chest at the gesture, and I can't help the smile that forms. Hadlee appears to be all sharp edges, but in truth, she's a cinnamon roll with gooey insides. I sigh, glancing at the time on my phone.

"I've got to get back to work," I say, adjusting the tight bodice of my dress. "I'll call you later?"

"Sure." She yawns again. "It's my day off, so whatever."

I laugh. "Okay. Love you, Lee."

"Love you too, Jay."

The line disconnects, but I stay in my spot. It's quiet here. Only the soft hum of fluorescent lights breaks the silence, but even that is better than the rumble of customer service agents talking over one another.

It's been months since I found my boyfriend cheating on me with his secretary, but some days it feels more painful than others. When he moved out of our shared apartment, I was sure that would be the end of it. No contact meant no more heartbreak—right? *Wrong.*

Up until last week, George had continued to pay his half of the rent. Two days ago, he told me he couldn't anymore. He moved in with the secretary—Jessica—and can't spare the funds. Now, rent is due in a week, and I'm floundering to pull enough funds together to make it work.

The lease lasts for another two months, and I have no idea how I'm supposed to make it work with my pittance of an income.

I groan, dropping my head into my hands.

When did life become so difficult?

The moment I step out of the bathroom, I mentally curse myself for wearing a dress to work. Not only are my thighs chafing, but the office perv, Greggory, hasn't taken his eyes off me. I try to ignore the sleazy leer he sends me as I walk past his cubicle, but it's physically impossible. The slime is palpable.

My phone is ringing when I make it back to my desk, but as I slide into my chair, it goes silent. I groan, noticing my boss glaring at me from his office. He's always looking for a reason to yell, and I'm pretty sure I just gave him one.

"Thomas!" he shouts, not even bothering to come to the door. His pudgy face is flushed a deep pink, his brows furrowed over tiny eyes. I push myself up and adjust my skirt before walking toward his office. Closing the door behind me, I try to brace myself for the timebomb that is Darryl Hansen.

I perch on the edge of the red vinyl chair, hating how my skirt rides up my legs, bringing his beady eyes to my thighs. His tongue swipes over his chapped lips and I swallow back the bile rising in my throat. My heart beats quickly, anxiety crawling up my spine as I wait for his eyes to move back to my face.

"Your phone has been ringing off the hook, yet you've barely answered it," he says, letting his eyes drag slowly up my body. I try not to move, fighting not to shudder under his sickening gaze. "Why is that?"

I bite the inside corner of my mouth and take a deep breath in through my nose, regretting it instantly. Darryl's office smells like an awful mixture of Axe body spray and body odor, and I choke on my breath. I try to cover it by coughing into my fist, but his slimy grin morphs into a glare. His brow furrows and his face darkens two shades.

"I've answered every call directed to my line as it came in," I answer finally, tucking a stray curl behind my ear. I clasp my hands in my lap, trying to keep the tremor of anxiety from showing. "I was coming back from a short break when that last call came in, and I missed it."

"You don't take this job seriously," he says, and I clench my jaw in frustration. The leer is back, but now it has an arrogant overtone.

I don't get paid enough to take this job seriously, I think angrily. "Sir, I understand it may seem that way, but I assure you, I take my job *very* seriously."

"Unfortunately, the company doesn't see that reflected in your work," Darryl says, stepping around his desk and towering over me. The smell gets stronger as he moves closer, and I breathe through my mouth to dampen it.

"What do you mean?" I ask, squirming in my seat. His eyes trail over me again, and my skin crawls. I can't focus on anything with this putrid scent overwhelming my senses and making my eyes water. And his borderline sexual harassment isn't helping either.

"We've decided to let you go, Thomas." His voice is thick, and I stare up at him in shock. His eyelids droop as he smirks down at me.

"You're *firing* me?" I ask incredulously. *This can't be happening.*

"I've been handed down orders from the higher-ups," he says, licking his lips again as his eyes drop to my cleavage. I fight the urge to fold my arms, knowing that will simply enhance the view. "Now, I could perhaps be...persuaded...to put a good word in for you. Maybe save your job—if you do something for me, of course."

My eyes drop from his face to where he fiddles with his belt, and I can't hide my disgust.

"Or I could get you fired for this entire encounter!" I say, pushing myself out of the chair. It's a mistake. me closer to him. His breath is hot and thick on my face, the smell of stale whiskey and mouthwash washing over me with every exhale. "Harassing an employee, drinking on the job—"

"You've got nothing, Thomas," he hisses, pushing his face closer. I lean back, feeling queasy. "No one is gonna do a thing about any of that—I'm the only manager they've been able to keep. You think they're gonna listen to a little nobody like you? I'm trying to help you. All you gotta do is put that pretty little mouth to work—"

Crack!

My hand collides with his cheek. His face flashes from surprise to fury quicker than I can blink, and his fingers wrap tightly around my wrist.

"Please pack your desk and be off the premises before noon," he says, his voice cold and even. My stomach plummets, and I stumble back when he shoves me away. I let my feet carry me from the room and back to my desk. Not only had I been propositioned by my boss, but I'd been fired.

Fired. I was fired.

Hadlee was right—it was time to go home. Not that I had much choice in the matter. After the unfortunate turn of events at the office, there was no way I could pay my rent on time. The only good thing to come from the whole thing was getting Darryl fired too.

Getting out of my lease had taken the most effort. I had everything packed in two suitcases within hours of being fired, but it took longer to convince the landlord. Four days and two loaves of fresh baked bread later, he finally caved and let me out of the lease. After that, I bought a one-way ticket back to Montana.

As I take my first steps out of the airport, I pull my windbreaker tighter around my body. The winter air is chilly, and the lightweight fabric does little to keep me warm. I brace myself against the soft winds and walk further out into the cold. Snow falls in what feels like slow motion as I take in the beauty of the snowcapped mountains before me.

Montana winters are beautiful, if nothing else.

A familiar figure bounces beside a bright orange Subaru, and I can't fight the smile that pulls to my lips. Warmth floods my chest when Hadlee squeals, running toward me wrapped in the biggest coat I've ever seen. Her dark hair pokes out of her hat, and I can barely see her smile behind the scarf wrapped tightly around her neck.

"Jana!" She throws her arms around me, squeezing me in a tight, warm hug. I don't know whether to laugh or cry as the weight of anxiety lifts from my shoulders. I hadn't realized how disconnected I've been over the last few years until I hug her back, relishing the feeling of human contact. "I'm so happy you're home!"

"Me too, Lee," I say, pulling back just enough to see her face. I brush her hair from my mouth and laugh. Despite everything that's led me to this moment, I'm glad to be back, to feel the warmth of friendship and love. Tugging my suitcases closer, I peer around us once more. "I forgot how much it snows out here."

"You must be freezing!" Her eyes dart over my full figure, taking in my leggings and college sweatshirt beneath the lightweight jacket. Her grip on my shoulders tightens and she frowns. "Did you bring a better coat?"

I shake my head with a shrug.

"I didn't need anything more than this back in Louisiana," I say as she takes one of my bags and leads me to the waiting Subaru. I watch her struggle to heft the suitcase into the trunk with a grin. I only fight a little with the second suitcase as I shove it in next to hers. "Come to think of it, this is *heavier* than anything I could've worn in Louisiana."

"I can't even imagine living out there, Jay," Hadlee says shaking her head. She slams the hatch before hurrying around the car. I follow her lead, climbing into the passenger seat. Warmth seeps into my body as I settle into my seat, buckling up before letting my hands hover in front of the vents. The heater slowly defrosts my frozen fingertips. "The humidity alone would've wreaked havoc on my hair."

"You're right—" Looking over at her as she strips off her hat and overcoat, I grin. Her sleek black hair wouldn't have lasted a day in the New Orleans humidity. "You'd be doomed out there. My hair was curlier than ever though."

"Oh, I bet!" She glances at me, her green eyes calculating. I swipe my hand over the unruly mess, sure the snow destroyed any semblance of order the curls once had. "I love your curls so much, Jay."

I roll my eyes but smile anyway. "God, I missed you."

"Of course you did," she says, flipping her hair over her shoulder with a smirk. "I'm a delight."

We both laugh.

"Jokes aside," she says, reaching across the console and squeezing my hand. "I missed you, too. It's just not been the same without you here."

I squeeze her hand three times in return, earning a small smile. It's been six years since I was last in Harmony. Despite the lapse, it felt like no time had passed between us. *Just like always.*

Hadlee pulls out of the pick-up line, and I stare out the window as we pass a row of parked cars. My heart aches at the sight of reuniting families; parents hold their children tightly with tears in their eyes, and couples embrace passionately on the sidewalk. The ache is familiar, though less than the last time I felt it.

Nothing has felt as strong as the last time I was here—for my parents' funeral. Ever since, emotions have felt dampened, not quite real. Not even George's betrayal hurt as deeply as I expected it to.

I blink past the tears that have collected on my lashes, and mentally shake myself. *Now's not the time.* I push my parents from my mind. Instead, I focus on the Christmas music filtering from the radio as the car pulls away from the airport and out onto the freeway.

The drive back to Harmony takes just under an hour, and Hadlee fills my silence with stories of the salon she works at and the people around town. I don't hear much of what she says, though; my mind is stuck on the betrayals of George and my boss, both of whom tore through my delicately balanced sanity and left me a mess.

I rest my head on the window as I watch the trees fly past, and it's not until I see the town limits that I perk up.

Harmony, Montana
Where you're family
Population: 856

"Oh, I ran into Mrs. F the other day and told her you were moving back." Hadlee's words ring in my ears and it takes me a moment to register them.

Mrs. Filly—lovingly called Mrs. F by the locals—has owned the Little Button Bakery since it opened in 1982. I worked for her my entire high school career, right up until I left for college.

"She said you have a job if you want it."

"Really?" I ask, my interest piqued. Ever since I was little, I've loved baking. It was my passion from the moment my mom showed me how to make brownies at six. When I got my degree in business management, I had dreamed of opening my own little bakery one day.

"Yeah, *really*."

"I've been itching to get back into baking," I say wistfully. "George hated it when I baked. You know what a health freak he was—constantly talking about how if I just made changes to my diet, I could lose the extra weight."

"Are you kidding?" Hadlee looks furious. "I swear to God, I'm gonna kill him next time I see him."

Since we grew up together, Hadlee is one of the only people to know about my struggle with my weight. I've always been on the heavier side, and it took almost starving myself to death to come to the realization that I don't need to be skinny to love myself.

"It's okay," I say, brushing my hair away from my face. "He's not worth going to jail for."

"I agree." She peers at me with a wicked grin. "I never said I would get caught, though."

"I'm okay, Lee," I say with a laugh. "Promise."

"Okay, fine." She sighs, tapping her fingers on the steering wheel. "Do you want to swing by the bakery to make it official?"

"Yeah, I think that's a great idea. Besides," I grin at her, "I'm famished after my flight."

CHAPTER TWO
ALEX

The chilly winter air whips around me as I rush to get my daughters out of the backseat of my truck. Maddie unbuckles her car seat easily as I struggle with the harness on Morgan's. My oldest watches me, irritation clear on her face.

"Daddy, it's freezing!" she whines, as if I'm not standing in the cold myself. "Hurry up!"

I lift an eyebrow, but my fingers continue trying to free my dozing five-year-old. "Is that how we talk?"

Maddie juts out her chin, a pout forming. She's developed more of an attitude in the last year, and it drives me insane when it's directed at me. *Seven going on seventeen.*

"Can we go inside, *please*?" she says, tilting her head innocently and giving me her best puppy dog eyes. "It's so cold out today."

"I'm working on it, Mads. Put your coat on." Morgan's seatbelt comes loose, and I untangle her limbs from the chair before picking her up. She curls into me, burying her face in my neck as the cold air hits her full force. A soft whine escapes her as I grab her coat from the floor and wrap it around her shoulders. I wait for Maddie to pull on her own coat before moving out of the doorway. "Alright, let's go."

I help Maddie jump down from the running board before ushering her up the stairs. Fumbling with the keys, I manage to open the shop with limited whining from the girls. The small bell tinkles as the door is shoved open by my impatient seven-year-old, then again as the door closes behind us. It's dark inside the bookshop, but Maddie quickly remedies that as we step inside. Flipping a switch on the wall, she watches in awe as the lights flicker on throughout the store. I set Morgan on the couch near the front window before gathering the mail from the porch.

"Daddy?" Morgan's soft voice fills the silence of the bookstore, and I turn to look at her. She rubs her sleepy eyes and smiles sweetly at me, warming my heart. "Are we gonna get pretty lights?"

I look around, distracted enough that I'm not sure what she's talking about. She hurries to the window, Maddie following, and they press their noses to the glass.

"Like the rest of the shops, Daddy," Maddie says, pointing to the street. I sigh, glancing down at the pile of mail in my hands.

"I don't know, girls," I say, my attention now caught on the white envelope with *PAST DUE* in big, bold, red letters. *Another bill.* I drop the pile onto the counter and run a hand through my hair.

"I want lights," Morgan cries. Big crocodile tears well up in the corners of her eyes. "They look like twinkling fairies."

"*Daddy*," Maddie joins her sister with that same look she gave me in the truck. I sigh again, taking in her crossed arms and disapproving frown. "It's almost Christmas, and we don't even have a *tree* yet."

"We *are* getting a tree...*right*, Daddy?" Morgan asks, smearing a tear across her chubby cheek. Her amber eyes, exact replicas of mine, light up in delight at the thought. "Mama loved decorating the tree."

I catch my breath at the mention of Laura, my heart breaking a little. Morgan is right—she *loved* decorating the tree. She loved Christmas in general, which is why I hate it so much. But despite my resolve not to decorate, I can't deny the hopeful glint in their eyes. "Sure, we can get a tree."

Their chorus of excitement fills the bookshop, and I can't help the smile that blooms as they clasp hands and dance in a circle. After Laura died, I promised I would strive to keep the light of joy in their lives. *A tree won't hurt anything.*

The bell above the door rings again, calling our attention to the customer stepping inside. The familiar face holds a playful grin. Pulling his winter hat off, he tousles his dark brown curls with a free hand before barking a cheerful, "Hello, family!"

The black dog at his feet echoes his sentiment with a playful bark but stays seated beside her owner.

"Uncle Benji!" The girls clamor over themselves to reach my brother, and he drops to his knees to welcome their hugs. I don't miss the slight wince as his knee hits the floor, but he covers it quickly with another wide grin.

"What's this?" he asks in amazement, holding Morgan at arm's length. I roll my eyes at his antics as she giggles, waiting for him to continue, and I catch Maddie mimicking my reaction. "You've grown so much since I saw you last."

"You saw us last night, Uncle Benji," Maddie reminds him, giving her attention to the pup. She scratches between her ears and under her chin, ignoring Morgan as she dissolves into a fit of laughter.

"You, Miss Madeline, are giving more love to Harper than to your favorite uncle," Benji notes, raising an eyebrow. Maddie fights a smile, placing kisses on the dog's muzzle.

"That's because I love her more," my seven-year-old sasses back, tossing her brown curls over her shoulder. A laugh slips past my lips as Benji frowns playfully.

"You *what*?" he says, grabbing her around the middle and pulling her onto his lap. She squeals, laughter filling the room as he begins to tickle her. "You love my dog more than me?"

"Yes!" she says through her laughter, pushing at his hands. "Harper is better than you!"

"Take that back!"

"Never!"

Turning my attention back to the pile of mail in front of me, I tuck the bills under a book and feign interest in the junk mail. I listen half-heartedly to their tickle fight, but my mind is locked on the reality of my situation. *I could lose the shop.*

I'm distracted, my eyes out of focus until Maddie finally flings her arms around Benji's neck and places a big, wet kiss on his cheek. "I love you, Benji."

"Good," he says, grinning down at her. "I love you too, Miss Madeline."

She rolls her eyes at the nickname but pushes out of his arms and grabs her sister's hand. "Come on, Morg. Let's go play princesses in the reading nook."

My phone rings as I watch them disappear into the back of the store. Still distracted, I pull it out of my back pocket and glance at the screen. I groan as my eyes focus on the name scrolling across it: Leslie. *My sister-in-law.*

I hit ignore as I turn to face my brother. "What are you doing here, Benj?"

He pushes to his feet, the wince more pronounced as he puts more weight on his injured knee. Harper leans against his legs as he rights himself, offering her counterweight. Despite the teasing, I agree with Maddie. Harper is absolutely the best. She came into our lives shortly after Benji moved to Harmony five years ago, and she's been invaluable to him since.

I turn my attention to the computer beside me, pretending I didn't see his struggle. I know from experience he won't appreciate my concern. Harper's the only one he'll accept help from.

Benji makes his way over to the counter and leans on his forearms with Harper at his feet.

"You've been mighty uptight lately, Lexi," he says, fiddling with the stack of business cards beside the register. I swat his hand away with a scowl.

"Don't call me that, Benjamin."

"What?" He smirks, standing to his full height to tower over me. "Uptight? Or Lexi?"

"Either, thanks."

"Aw, come on, Alex," he says, tapping his fingers on the countertop. The dull *thunk* of his fingers against the wood is enough to drive me nuts.

"No, you *come on*, Ben," I snap. He lifts a brow, curling his lips in. I sigh and run a hand through my dark hair before turning my attention to the computer. I watch the screen, waiting for it to load. "What are you doing here?"

"Can't I just visit my nieces?"

"Sure, you can," I say, glancing at him over the monitor. I know he's avoiding the subject; I just don't know what it is this time. "Which is why you swung by the house last night for movie night."

I watch the muscles in his jaw work as he studies me.

"I thought I could help out with the books." He admits, looking pointedly at the bills I tucked haphazardly beneath the stack of geography books when he walked in.

"Oh, *no*, Ben," I say, waving a hand in dismissal. "There's no need."

"Alex, I know the store has been struggling since Laura passed." He reaches for the papers and, despite my swatting hands, pulls them across the counter. "It's not a big deal, Alex. This is what I went to school for. It's *literally* what I do for a living."

Embarrassment floods me, and I scowl at my brother. He doesn't notice, though, since his eyes are busy scanning the bills and shipment invoices.

Logically, I know he's simply trying to help. He's right—the store *has* been floundering for the last two years without Laura's patient, guiding hand. A wave of regret rolls over me as I scan the rows of bookshelves. This place was Laura's dream—I can't sit idly by and let it die without a fight.

"Fine, you can look over the books," I say, picking up the stack of geography books and walking around the counter. "But I can't pay you."

"No worries, brother." Benji grins as he trades places with me so he can use the computer. "You can pay me by going out— get a date or something."

I shake my head, walking toward the back of the shop. The thought of going out with someone new sets alarms off in my head. Laura has been, and always will be, the only one for me. "I'm not dating, Benj."

"Are you sure?" he asks, staring at the computer screen now. His brow furrows as he compares something on the monitor to the papers in his hands. "You could get out, have a bit of fun—and by that, I mean *adult* fun."

"I don't need *adult* fun, Ben," I reply, glaring at the shelves in front of me. "I need to raise my daughters and keep Laura's dream alive."

"Do you really think Laura would want you to close yourself off from love?" His voice follows me to the non-fiction section, where I begin stacking the new books. I shake my head. Benji has always been one to bounce back from disaster, to find the light at the end of the tunnel, so to speak. But even two years isn't enough time to heal a heart from the loss of love. "And what about the girls? Don't they deserve a woman in their lives? Maddie is seven, but it's only a matter of time before she's going to need a woman around to help her through the changes of puberty."

"I'm not going to replace Laura just because you think I need to get laid, Ben."

"I'm not saying you need to replace Laura." His voice is soft and close. When I stand and turn, he's there, leaning against the shelf with his arms crossed. "I would never suggest that, Alex. I know how much you loved her."

"Love," I correct him. "I *love* Laura. That's not going away."

"I don't think it needs to. All I'm saying is that you should think about it." He glances over my shoulder, and I follow his gaze to the children's corner. Maddie and Morgan are sitting together, reading a book quietly. "Your girls need a mom, Alex."

CHAPTER THREE
JANA

"Thanks for all your help this morning, Jana," Mrs. Filly says, leaning across the table and clasping my hand. I offer a wide smile, gently squeezing her fingers.

"Of course!" I say, pushing unruly curls away from my face with my free hand. Despite the chill in the air, the bakery is humid, and my hair is a frizzy mess. "Thank you again for giving me a job last minute! I don't know what I would do if it wasn't for you, Mrs. F."

"Oh, sweet Jana," she coos, her kind blue eyes softening on a wrinkled face. "You were my best employee. I was so sad to lose you when you left for college."

"I've missed it here," I admit, letting my eyes drift around the small bakery. The last time I was here was for my parents' wake, and not a thing has changed in all these years. It still has the same off-white walls and old display case, the same checked flooring and mismatched tables and chairs. The only real difference is the kitchen appliances in the back.

"How long has it been?" she asks softly.

"Six years," I say, letting my eyes rest on the collection of photos littering the back wall. I don't have to see them up close to know at least three are images of my parents.

"Well, we're glad you've come home, sweetie."

Home. The word settles in my bones, raising the hairs on the back of my neck and causing my stomach to knot. My fingers itch to tap against the linoleum tabletop, but I pull my hands into my lap and clasp them together to fight the urge.

I don't have a home—not anymore.

"I should really be going." I smile as I push myself out of the chair and adjust my jacket. "Hadlee asked me to pick up some pinecones from the store on my way home."

The lie slips out easily, and Mrs. F doesn't bat an eyelash. She smiles brightly and nods. "Ah, well, have a lovely afternoon, Jana—and say hello to Hadlee for me."

"I will. Thank you, Mrs. F," I reply, heading for the door. "I'll see you tomorrow."

"See you tomorrow, sweetie."

I leave the warmth of the bakery and pull my jacket tighter around my body. I still need to pick up a new coat, but first, I need to get a thank-you gift for Hadlee. When she invited me to stay with her, I was worried about putting her out. Luckily, her beautiful house not only has a guest room for me, but it has its own ensuite bathroom as well.

Walking down Main Street, I take in the beauty and charm of Harmony. The rows of shops hold true to their small-town roots, made of red brick with big glass windows framed in wrought iron. Snow lines the streets, the wrought iron streetlamps a stark contrast against the bright white. Snowflakes fall slowly, almost lazily, while Christmas lights glint in the gray of the afternoon.

I smile, nostalgia crashing through me. I used to wander these streets every day, visiting the shops, seeing films at the theater, and just enjoying life. Six years is a long time, but it feels like just yesterday.

The storefronts are all decorated with lights and garlands and bright red bows, and my heart warms at the sight. Six Christmases without snow—how did I ever live that way?

I continue down the street, looking for the bookstore. Hadlee has always loved books more than anything. In elementary school, we bonded over our love of fantasy novels— it was one of the reasons we're still such good friends.

I stop short in surprise when I see the bookstore across the street. It's in the same spot as the little bookstore from my childhood, but there's an utter lack of decorations, not even lights in the windows. The new owners have renamed the old store—it's no longer *Ivers Books*, but *Brooks Books*.

Despite the lack of familiarity, I hurry across the street and open the shop's door. A cold burst of wind follows me in, mussing my hair and scattering a few pages on the counter. Two men stand behind the desk, and both look up at my entrance. My heart flops, my stomach somersaulting at the unexpected attention.

"Welcome in!" the taller of the two says, ruffling his dark curls as he grins at me. I smile back, stepping further into the building. They've reorganized the store, to the point where I'm not sure I'll be able to find what I need. There's a cute little reading area in front of the window display, just across from the checkout counter, with comfortable-looking armchairs and raw wood end tables. A black dog lying on one chair lifts its head from where it rests on big paws, tail wagging as it studies me.

I smile at the pup, resisting the urge to pet the floppy ears. Instead, I continue to look around. The displays are expertly organized, and there are fewer shelves than I remember *Ivers* having. *Oh God, I hope they have something Hadlee will like.*

"Are you looking for something specific?"

"Oh, um...yes, and no?" I say. A laugh pours from my lips, my cheeks heating in embarrassment. It's an absurd answer, and the man who has yet to say a word smirks a little. I swallow nervously, letting my eyes dance over the shelves nearest me. "Do you have any cute Christmas romances?"

"Yes!" the tall one says, his smile never faltering. "Alex here can show you where they are."

I stand awkwardly, waiting patiently as they have a silent conversation. The shop is oddly quiet, and glancing around, it appears that we're the only ones here. *Odd*. The taller man pushes the other one—Alex—out from behind the counter, and he stumbles a little before righting himself. I offer him a gentle smile, and he returns it with a furrowed brow and a scowl. He stalks forward, skirting around me.

"They're over here." His voice is rough, as if he hasn't used it in a while, and he clears his throat, his eyes darting to mine briefly before he looks away again. He cuts his fingers through his dark hair, and I smile at his awkwardness. *He's kind of adorable*. When he passes by, his cologne whispers around me—it's woodsy, with a hint of orange citrus. I follow him around a bookshelf, only to almost run into him when he stops abruptly.

"I couldn't help but notice you haven't decorated the storefront for Christmas," I say, trying to make small talk as he scans the shelves. He flicks his amber gaze my way, irritation evident in their depths.

"That's right."

His sharp response has my hackles rising, and I clench my teeth to keep from biting out a harsh reply. I inhale deeply, relaxing my shoulders and jaw on the exhale.

"I didn't mean to offend you," I say calmly, letting my eyes drift over the titles on the shelf.

"Then why say anything?" he asks, sidestepping and dropping to a crouch.

"Because," I bite out, already regretting the words, "your shop is the only one not lit up and decorated for the happiest time of year, though now I can see why."

"Oh, you can?" he asks, glaring harshly at me. "I suppose you're going to share that unasked-for opinion too?"

"What the hell is your problem?"

"*My* problem?" he scoffs, shaking his head and walking back toward the front of the store without showing me where the damned Christmas books are. I follow on his heels, furious with his attitude. "You come in here and immediately start criticizing my business, and you have the balls to ask me what *my* problem is?"

"No need to get your boxers in a twist," I mutter. He rounds on me, his eyes burning with anger. I sigh, annoyed, but stand my ground. *Way to go, Jana. Day one, and you've already pissed someone off.*

"I'm gonna ask you to leave," he says, the muscles in his jaw jumping.

"You're going to kick me out of your store for asking about Christmas lights?" I ask, my eyes widening. He gestures to the door, and I roll my eyes. "Can you really afford that?"

"Get the fuck out of my store!" he bellows. Narrowing my eyes at his tantrum, I step around him and hurry to the door. I turn back when I reach it and send him a heated glare.

"Merry Christmas to you too," I say, offering him my biggest smile before stepping out into the cold. The moment the door snaps shut behind me, I glare at the snow. "Asshole."

CHAPTER FOUR
ALEX

I watch the woman leave, frustration simmering in my veins. Her soft brown doe-eyes had been curious, her smile honest, but for some reason, it irked me. My gaze follows her trek down the road, and I immediately regret throwing her out in the cold like that.

Laura's voice fills my head. *What if someone treated Maddie or Morgan that way?* I would be furious. *So why would you treat a woman like that?*

I shake my head, focusing on the anger the woman had inspired. It was almost instantaneous. The moment she walked into the store, I was irritated—probably due to Benji's nagging, but also from the gust of wind that scattered the shipment invoices and logs. And then there was the silent look Benji had sent me, as if to say, *fate brought her.*

It wasn't just anger, though, and that scared me.

"Did you just kick her out?" Benji asks from behind me, the words ringing in my ears as if to mock me.

"Yes."

"Why the hell would you do that? She was your first customer." He echoes the woman's incredulous tone, and I sigh out a heavy breath as I close my eyes. I wipe a hand down my face, tired and frustrated by this whole situation.

"Does it really matter?" I ask, stepping around the counter. It's barely after one o'clock, but as Benji just pointed out, we haven't had a customer all day.

"Yes, *Alex*, it does matter." Benji's voice grates over my nerves, and I grip the countertop tightly. "You can't *afford* to be kicking people out. You're barely bringing in enough to keep the place open as it is."

The heartbreaking truth: Laura's bookshop dreams are spinning around the drain, and I can't figure out how to stop them from disappearing completely. This shop is the last connection my girls have to their mother and losing it would be like ripping her from their lives all over again. *I've got to figure this out.*

"I know," I mutter, glancing out the window again. The woman is gone, but she remains burned in my mind. Perhaps my reaction was harsh. She simply asked about the decorations—a similar question to the one the girls asked this morning—and I'd blown up at her.

The truth was, I was terrified. The moment my eyes landed on her I'd been unable to look away. Attraction, hot and overwhelming, rushed through me at the sight of her luscious curves and ruddy cheeks, and when she smiled…I was a goner. It was unexpected, not to mention confusing, especially following the conversation I'd just had with Benji. *I love Laura.*

"You know," Benji says, snapping my attention back to him. He's flipping through a book, his immediate attention not on me, but on the current statistics of killer whales. "Maybe you could host a book club or a weekly game night."

"A weekly game night?"

He lifts his head and shoots me a playful grin. "Yeah, like bingo or something."

"That's the worst idea you've ever had," I say with a small laugh, shaking my head as I begin closing out the register. "Although, a book club wouldn't be a horrible idea."

"Exactly."

"What I really need is to find the funds to hire a teenager to watch the register in the afternoons."

"That's a good idea," Benji says, tucking the book back on the shelf beside him. I lift a brow, counting the same bills I counted this morning. *No one has come in today except that woman. Why bother going through the motions?* "Do you have someone in mind?"

"Wren's brother, Zach," I say, noting the way he perks up at the mention of Wren. He's got it bad for my babysitter but refuses to admit it. "He's looking for an afterschool job, but I can't afford to pay him right now."

"I can help you move things around to free up enough for the kid," Benji says nonchalantly, shrugging his shoulders. I lift my brow again, trying to hide the smirk that plays on my face. Benji ignores me, glancing at his watch and frowning. "Are you seriously closing this early every day?"

"Yeah, I can't afford to keep it open later." I finish counting the till and lock it, pulling together my things before calling for the girls. "Besides, Maddie has ballet in the afternoons, and Morgan starts gymnastics soon. I don't have the time to man the counter all day."

The girls come running from the back, each clutching a book to their chest, pleading eyes already in place.

"Can we take these home with us, Daddy?" Maddie asks, her hazel-green eyes wide and her lashes fluttering. Morgan watches her sister for a moment before copying her expression, a silly grin peeking through her pout. Benji laughs, and I shoot him a glare.

"I'll work on freeing up the cash for Zach," he says, snapping his fingers to call for Harper. "You work on saying no to your daughters."

Benji's laughter follows him out the front door, but I ignore him. I look between my daughters, determined not to make one of them cry again.

"We have lots of books at home," I say, wrapping my scarf around my neck. I hold Maddie's jacket out to her, and she takes it with a frown.

"But we don't have *these* books at home," she reasons, tucking her coat under her arm and holding up the book she wants—a book about trains. I roll my eyes, not surprised in the least. She's been obsessed with trains since Laura bought one four years ago to run around the base of the tree. I shake my head and hold up Morgan's coat, attempting to get her to put her arms in.

"I really want *this* book, Daddy," Morgan says softly, her eyes trailing over the cover of the book in her little hands—*The Twelve Dancing Princesses*. My heart twinges, and I want to give in to their demands, but I know I can't. "It has lots of princesses in it."

"You know, girls," I say conspiratorially, crouching down in front of them and pulling them closer to me. "Christmas is in a couple weeks—why don't you ask Santa for them?"

"Santa's not *real*, Daddy," Maddie says matter-of-factly, and I almost choke on my tongue. *What?* I try to school my face, hoping my surprise isn't obvious. *Who the fuck told her that?*

"Santa's not real?" Morgan asks, her bottom lip trembling. I can already see tears brimming in her big brown eyes.

"Of course he is, sweetie." I glance at Maddie, her hazel-green eyes filling with tears too. My heart breaks at their disappointment and I'm ready to fight whoever told my seven-year-old Santa isn't real. This was *not* on my radar for this year, and I silently wonder what Laura would say to ease their fears. "Maddie, where did you hear that?"

"A boy at school," Maddie replies, wiping at her cheeks with the back of her hand.

"Do you believe him?"

I watch her face as she thinks. Her nose crinkles a little, her eyes narrowing as she tilts her head. She moves her lips back and forth, as though she has an itch she can't get with her hands full, the wheels turning in her head. I see the moment she makes a decision, her face relaxing into a smile.

"No."

"Do you believe in Santa?" I ask.

"Yes, Daddy."

"See, Morg?" I say with a smile, turning to the five-year-old. "Maddie knows Santa's real."

Relief floods through me as the tears are wiped away, replaced with smiles and laughter. They pull their coats on and set the books on the front counter, agreeing to write Santa the moment we arrive home. Ushering them out to the truck, I pray nothing else goes wrong this Christmas.

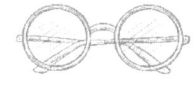

"Thanks for coming to watch them, Wren," I say, pulling my coat up over my shoulders. She smiles, her eyes glinting in the light from the TV. Maddie and Morgan sit transfixed on the couch, watching the claymation Santa Claus sing and dance.

"Of course, Alex," she says, cutting a hand through her blonde hair. It flops to one side, opening her face to be studied. While the smile is still in place, it doesn't reach her eyes. She looks tired, and as she cocks a shoulder to lean against the wall, I catch a glimpse of sadness in the depths of her eyes. "I love watching them."

"How's your mom?" I ask, shoving my hands into my pockets.

"She's been better," she says with a sigh, her eyes glossing with unshed tears. She crosses her arms and licks her lips. "I think this is gonna be her last Christmas."

My chest tightens, aching for her and the loss she's experiencing. It's different; losing someone suddenly like I did was unexpected, but Wren has to suffer watching her mother lose her mind, forgetting who she is and how much she's loved.

"I'm so sorry, Wren."

She smiles sweetly, sliding her hand through her hair again. It's a tick, something she does just to have something to do with her hands. "Thanks, Alex."

"I'll be back in an hour or so, depending on how long this meeting goes."

"No worries," she says, waving me toward the door. "I'll have them all tucked in and sleeping before you get back."

"Thank you." I wave as I step outside, hating that I have to go to this dumbass town hall meeting. Wren smiles as she closes the door behind me, and I sigh out an irritated breath. Laura used to love these meetings, and I loved going with her. Since her death, though, I've dreaded every single one.

I hurry to my truck, the cold biting at my exposed ears. My phone rings in my pocket and I fish it out as I close the door. Leslie's name flashes across the screen and I groan. *Take the hint and leave me alone!* I ignore the call again, slamming the phone onto the seat next to me.

It's been two years, and somehow seeing Laura's sister's name flash across my screen hurts worse each time I see it.

The phone rings again. I shove the keys into the ignition as I pick up the cell, pain and anger coursing through me. "What?"

"Is that how you answer phone calls?" Benji asks with a laugh. "No wonder people don't come into the store."

I roll my eyes at his pithy reply and contemplate hanging up on him. "What do you need, Ben?"

"Just thought you'd want to know I've moved some things around, and you now have enough money to hire Zach."

"Do I want to know?" I ask, backing out of the driveway. His voice fills the cab as I drive back into town. When we bought the house out here on the edge of town, the plan had been to raise chickens and maybe get some cows. Those plans died with my wife.

"It's nothing crazy," he assures me. The line goes quiet for a moment, and I can almost imagine him running a hand through his hair. "Have you thought more about that conversation from this morning?"

"The book club?" I ask, purposefully ignoring the real reason he called. I should've known he would follow up on my dating—or lack thereof.

"You know that's not what I'm talking about," he says with a sigh. "I can help you fill out a profile online—unless there's someone specific you'd like to go out with."

Luscious curves and big brown eyes flood my mind, and I clench my jaw, shaking my head as my blood heats. I haven't been able to get her out of my head since she walked out of my shop. "I already told you, Ben: I'm not interested in dating."

"I know what you said, but it's been two years."

"I know how long it's been, Benjamin," I bite out harshly, angry at him, but also at myself.

"I just want you to be happy," he insists, the line going silent again.

"I am happy," I say, despite the ache in my chest. I force a laugh. "I've got plenty of women in my life, Benj. They run it, even."

"Okay," he says, and I breathe out a sigh of relief. "I'll drop it if you promise to at least think about it."

"Sure," I lie, pulling up in front of Town Hall. "I'll think about it."

CHAPTER FIVE
JANA

I stare up at the red brick building, taking in the grandeur of the historic Town Hall. One thing's for sure: they knew what they were doing when they built Harmony. I'm almost positive every single building lining Main Street is original to the town.

I try to ignore the curious looks sent my way, recalling the conversation from half an hour ago. Mrs. Filly had called frantically, asking me to attend the town hall meeting in her place. Her grandson's wife was in labor, and she needed to get to the hospital in Missoula—three hours away.

Hadlee links her arm through mine, adjusting the hem of her dress as we walk across the street. I fiddle with my sweater, feeling obnoxiously underdressed beside my best friend.

"I thought this was just a town hall meeting," I mutter, taking in her sleek red dress and heels.

"It is," she says, smiling at someone who passes us. I clasp my hands together and tap my fingers against the back of my wrist as anxiety crawls up my spine. *Tap, tap, tap, tap.*

"Then why are you wearing a cocktail dress?"

"Because I work at a salon," she whispers, waving flirtatiously at someone else as we meander inside. "I never get to wear my fancy dresses anymore."

"Well, you could've told me to change," I say, letting my eyes drop to my feet.

"What's wrong with your outfit?" she asks, peering at my gray Columbia sweater, black leggings, and boots. "I think you look adorable, Jay."

"Oh, thanks," I say sarcastically, picking at a stray thread at my wrist. Hadlee pulls me to an abrupt stop, and I look at her in surprise as she takes my hands in hers.

"I don't know why you do that, but I'm serious." She cocks her head, a small smile gracing her lips. Her dark hair is pulled up in an effortless bun, her green eyes framed in dark lashes and liner. *She looks gorgeous, and I—* "You look adorable, Jana! Any guy here would be lucky to have you."

I snort.

"I'm done with men, Lee," I say, pushing my glasses up and glancing around the room. "I'm so sick of putting myself out there, I just want to go home. I've been cheated on—twice! Why would I willingly put myself through that again?"

"Not every guy out there is a cheater, Jay," Hadlee says. She gives me a look, something between pity and concern, as she smooths a hand down my arm. "Jon and George are a couple of assholes."

"All men are, Hadlee," I say, recalling the disaster at the bookstore. "I've just got to accept that and move on."

Hadlee sighs and links her arm through mine again. I allow her to drag me through the crush of people to a spot in the center of the room, and we take our seats. "Don't give up on finding love, Jana. You never know—your soulmate could be here in this very room."

I roll my eyes but laugh anyway. Hadlee Scott, ever the romantic. I let my eyes wander and take in my surroundings now that I don't feel like the center of attention. The room we're in is something akin to a theater with the most uncomfortable velvet chairs. At the head of the room is a stage with a long table set up in the center—no doubt where the mayor and chair-people will sit.

I continue to look around, people-watching really, when my eyes latch on to an oddly familiar figure. I lift a hand to my lips, gnawing on the cuticle of my thumb. *Of course he's here.* Dark curls fall into warm amber eyes—and there's that damn scowl again. At this point, I'm sure it's been permanently etched into that stupidly handsome face.

Alex.

I watch him scan the room, taking the chance to observe him from a distance. He's far too attractive to be a real grinch, despite the attitude I'd received at our first meeting. *Benefit of the doubt, and all*, I think.

It takes me a moment to realize his scowl has stopped on me.

I catch my breath, suddenly feeling *far* too warm. He holds eye contact a moment longer than appropriate, but his expression never changes. Traitorous butterflies erupt in my stomach, and I can't tear my gaze away. From this distance, I'm not sure if he took in my messy bun or college sweater, but I feel more uncomfortable anyway.

I drop my hands, tugging on the hem of the gray sweater. *Does he like what he sees? Is that why he's not looking away?*

"Why do you keep fiddling with your sweater like that?" Hadlee asks in a hushed whisper, swatting my hands away from the fabric.

"I'm self-conscious," I mutter, dragging my eyes from the handsome ass leaning against the wall. "I don't remember the last time I came to one of these meetings, and I feel like everyone is watching me."

It's not a lie. There's just a *specific* set of amber brown eyes that burn through me and won't seem to go away.

"No one is looking at you, Jay," she says in an attempt to soothe my nerves. I cross my arms, trying to ignore the heat of his glare and the curious glances from the people crowding into seats. *Disappear for six years, and this is what coming home gets you.* "Besides, you're just here to take notes for Mrs. F, which is so far from attention drawing, it's like living in a cave."

"I wish I was in a cave right now," I mutter, sinking lower in my chair.

"Oh, stop being such a spoilsport." Hadlee's brows furrow, and she turns her attention to the front of the room. "They're supposed to announce the Christmas festival tonight."

"Welcome!" a strong, deep voice echoes around the hall, and my eyes fly to the man standing on the stage beside the table. He's tall, with blond hair turning gray at the temples. It falls in soft waves over his forehead into bright eyes. His smile is blinding, and he tousles his hair with a hand before continuing. "If we could have everyone take a seat, we can begin!"

The crowd settles, seats filling quickly and the din quieting. I fish out my phone, planning to take notes with it, but a notification stops me in my tracks.

georgieborge has posted a new photo—view now!

My chest feels tight as my thumb hovers over the notification, my mind racing. I haven't heard from George in two weeks, and before that, we hadn't spoken in three months. I glance at Hadlee, but she's focused on the man on stage. *What's the harm in checking?*

The moment the app loads, I regret it. *Harm! Lots of harm!*

It's a photo of George, tanned skin on display, standing behind the pretty blonde secretary I caught him banging on the back of my couch. His arms are wrapped around her shoulders, and she clasps his hands. They're both grinning ear to ear, standing on a beach somewhere.

The sound of the meeting fades to nothing, and all I can seem to hear is the buzz of fluorescent lights. My breathing becomes shallow, and I can't look away from the disaster my life has become. George never took me anywhere. We stayed in more often than not, and anytime I suggested an outing, he looked horrified by the thought.

Seeing him with her—with *Jessica*—all the work I've done in the last three months to get over him unravels. I should've known the moment he hired her that this would happen, but I was in a blissful bubble, only seeing what he wanted me to see.

I clench my jaw, my grip on the phone tightening as tears of anger begin to blur my vision.

"I thought you blocked him," Hadlee hisses, taking my phone and tucking it into her clutch purse. She gestures to the front of the room, where the handsome blond man is speaking. I shake my head, wiping the dampness from my eyes with the sleeve of my sweater. "Now's not the time for a George-related meltdown, Jay."

"I'm sorry, I couldn't help it—I just opened the app."

"I will block him for you," she says softly, her eyes searching my face. "Now, I need you to focus. This is why we're here—Mayor Bradley just announced the local stores are teaming up for booths this year."

"That should be interesting," I say, not interested at all.

"Now," the man—Mayor Bradley—says, holding up a bowl. "We've already written the local business names on a strip of paper and placed them in this bowl. I'll draw two names, and those businesses will be paired for a booth. Sound good?"

There's a cacophony of agreement, and he reaches his hand into the bowl. "Casey's Cuts and Feldman's."

Hadlee groans, sinking back into her chair. "Feldman's? They're the worst to be paired with."

"Why? Because it's a hardware store, or because little Frankie Donnelly works there?"

She shoots daggers my way, and I laugh despite myself.

"They're the worst because they're a hardware store. What's our booth going to be—who can nail a board faster?" her brows furrow, her bright red lips pinching into a scowl. "Besides, Frank Donnelly hasn't lived in Harmony in four years, Jana."

Frankie was two years younger than Hadlee and me, and he had the biggest crush on my best friend in high school. His attention bordered on stalking, but I never thought he was dangerous. Her comment about him leaving four years ago is curious, but before I can ask more about it, Mayor Bradley's voice echoes through the hall again.

"Little Button Bakery," he says, pausing as he reaches for the second name. This is what I came for, the reason Mrs. F needed me to attend the meeting at all. *Who are we partnered with?* "And Brooks Books!"

My jaw drops, and I swing my gaze across the room to where Alex stands, irritation clear on his face. *This cannot be happening right now.*

CHAPTER SIX
JANA

Setting the needle arm onto a new record, I wait until the soft strains of Bing Crosby's *'Silent Night'* play through the house before walking back into the kitchen. I wash my hands and spread a fresh layer of flour across the quartz countertop. A chill seeps into the room despite the heat rolling from the oven, and I adjust the sleeves of my sweater before dumping the bowl onto the counter.

I press my fingers into the sugary mix, enjoying the sticky sensation as it creeps into every crevice of my hands. The motion of kneading dough relaxes me, more on my mind than I care to admit. Lifting a hand, I wipe at an itch on my forehead with the back of my wrist.

My eyes dart up, landing briefly on the box of abandoned decorations by the couch. *We still need a tree*. I sigh. My usual cheer and excitement for Christmas is severely lacking this year, and I can only attribute it to George's betrayal.

I smack the dough roughly as a tear slips down my cheek.

"These cookies aren't going to bake themselves," I mutter, wiping my cheek on my shoulder. Sniffling, I start pressing the sugar cookie dough flat before I reach out and wrap my sticky fingers around the rolling pin. It's not like I've got anything better to do than bake.

I roll the dough with extra force, my mind stuck on the series of photos George posted this weekend. All of them were taken during their island vacation, all captioned with the words "***anniversary weekend with my love***". It makes me sick, knowing they were together for half of my relationship with him.

Every late night, every work trip, every excuse he ever made—they were all for her. He refused to take me places, because she was more important. I smack the counter hard, the betrayal and fury rushing through me at full force. The door swings open, and I lift my head, meeting Hadlee's startled gaze.

"Are you angry baking again?" she asks, pushing the door closed with her foot and tossing her keys into the small bowl on the entryway table. I sigh, relinquishing my tight grip on the rolling pin. Instead, I grab a cookie cutter and smack it into the dough. Hitting things feels therapeutic, and the tension begins

Healing with You

to drain from my shoulders as I continue the motions. Hadlee toes off her heels, holding a brown paper bag out as a peace offering. "I brought Chinese."

I gnaw on my cheek, debating my next move. Baking is relieving the anger, but I haven't eaten anything for hours. Hadlee raises a brow, noting my hesitation.

"Come eat and tell me what's got your panties in a bunch," she says, moving into the living room. I snort, shaking my head, but I move to the sink anyway. I scrub the lingering dough from my hands and sigh, my shoulders sinking as I remember exactly *what* started this entire pity party.

"The mail."

Hadlee sets the bag of food on the table and picks up the offending piece of mail as she drops onto the couch. I grab a bottle of merlot before moving to the cabinet and getting out two wine glasses. I hear her growl lowly, and a smile pulls at my lips at her disgust. I move around and drop into the seat beside her, offering her a glass. She takes it, her brow furrowed, and her lips pursed in anger.

I already know the words written there by heart.

You are cordially invited to the wedding of Jessica Leigh Halstaff and George Earl Lomby March 14th.

"This is low, even for that asshole," she says, tossing her glossy black hair over her shoulder. She tears the cream-colored paper in half and drops it to the coffee table. She shakes her head and starts pulling boxes out of the bag.

I fiddle with the wine bottle, struggling to open it with my mind elsewhere. George and I had dated for two years, and I genuinely thought I would marry him—until I walked in on him fucking Jessica over the back of the couch I bought. It was then I realized he'd been cheating on me for the second half of our relationship.

"What is *wrong* with me?" I ask, pressure building behind my eyes for the third time today. Hadlee takes the wine and pops it open, pouring us each a glass before turning to face me. "Am I just...unlovable?"

"You're not unlovable, Jay," she says softly, pushing curls away from my face. Her green eyes hold sympathy—pity, even. "George is an idiot."

"Okay, so George is an idiot," I say, dropping my face into my hands. I can't argue with her statement, because George *is* an idiot. But Jon wasn't. Jon was a pre-med student with aspirations to be a surgeon. He was the smartest guy I knew—and I was the idiot. "What about Jon? We dated for three years. *Three fucking years*, Lee, and what do I have to show for *that* relationship? Fucking trust issues, that's what."

"Who sleeps with their TA anyway?" I know she's trying to make me feel better, but I can't keep the tears from spilling over, even as a laugh pours from me. Hadlee pats my back softly. "Jon was an idiot too, Jay."

I lift my head, dashing the traitorous tears away, and reach for my glass. I swish the red liquid around in the glass, trying to ignore the way my heart sinks in my chest. I bite the inside of my cheek and look up at her. "So, what? I just have terrible taste in men?"

"You just haven't found *the one* yet," she says, rubbing soothing circles over my back. She's watching me with that look—the one that screams *poor Jana*.

"*The one?*" I bite out a belittling laugh, angry at myself for being so weak, so vulnerable. I used to believe in soulmates, in finding the person you were meant to be with, someone who would get you on a whole other level. Sitting here with a broken heart and the soft strains of Bing Crosby playing in the background, I'm not so sure anymore. "Maybe there's no such thing."

"Just give it some time." Hadlee sounds so certain that I nod, allowing her words to assure me. "You'll find him."

Quinn Shields, assistant manager at Little Button and an old friend from high school, studies me when I walk into the bakery a few days later. She cocks her head, her fiery red ponytail swishing with the movement and her brown eyes calculating.

"Mrs. F is still out of town," she says, her jaw working as she chews her bubble gum. She blows a bubble the size of her face, letting it pop loudly in the deserted break room. "She said they've been snowed in up there and she doesn't know when—or if—she'll be back this winter."

I shrug off my coat and hang it in my locker, fishing out my apron. "Okay, so what does that mean for the shop?"

Quinn sits at the table, her legs crossed, and her arms folded. She smiles, shaking her head. "Not really sure. I guess I've got to keep it running, and *someone* is gonna have to take over the festival assignment for me."

My eyes widen, and I shake my head. I'd gratefully passed that assignment off to her when I'd learned about it, and there was no way I would take it back. One encounter with the grinch was more than enough for me.

"I'll do anything else, Q," I say, dropping into the chair across from her. "I'll clean the donut fryers for a month."

My friend laughs, her eyes twinkling with mischief. "Hadlee said you need to get out of the kitchen and into the light, and I agree. It's easy to wallow in your feelings back here."

"I swear, I'm not wallowing."

Sure, I've been a bit depressed since finding out that not only had George taken his mistress on my dream vacation, but had apparently grown enough balls to marry her too. Who wouldn't be? But that had nothing to do with why I wanted to stay as far from the Christmas festival booth as I could possibly get.

"I beg to differ," Quinn says, twirling her ponytail around a finger. She studies me for a few minutes longer before leaning forward conspiratorially. "Jan, you're depressed, and we're worried about you. Even Wren has noticed, and she's hardly been around lately."

"Wren has her own shit to deal with," I reply, tucking a stray curl behind my ear.

"I know that," Quinn says softly. She leans back and sighs. "But she cares about you, and she's concerned. Despite what she's going through with her mama, she's still your friend."

"I know," I whisper. I feel terrible knowing my issues have caused Wren more stress than she's already under.

"Look," Quinn says, drumming her perfectly manicured nails on the table. "I'm putting you on the booth—at least for now."

Panic seizes in my chest. Not only is the idea of overseeing something so obviously important to the community horrifying, but I have no desire to buddy up with the only man in town who apparently *hates* Christmas. "Do I have to?"

"Yes."

"I would really rather work in the bakery, Quinn," I say. She smirks but shakes her head.

"And I'd love to go to Tahiti for Christmas," she says, pushing to her feet as Polly walks in. Her dark eyes dart between us, and she hurries past to drop her stuff in her locker before heading into the kitchen. Quinn's brown eyes glint as she pushes the bright pink bubblegum through her lips and blows another bubble. It deflates with a loud snap, and she smiles devilishly at me. "Unfortunately, we don't always get what we want."

I sigh, irritated. My friends have no idea about the disastrous interaction with Alex from my first day back, and I really wasn't going to tell them. I open my mouth, ready to explain the horrible situation when she says something that stops me.

"Just make sure you don't mess it up." The teasing glint is gone, a serious look on her normally playful face. "Mrs. F will never admit this, but The Button isn't doing great. We need things to go perfectly at the festival, or there's a chance she could lose the store."

Standing outside Brooks Books, I glare harshly at the neon light in the window proclaiming they're open. This is not how I was planning to spend my afternoon, yet here I am. Sometime after the lunch rush, Quinn had pushed me out the door with instructions to 'take care of the booth'.

Cold air whips around me, threatening to freeze me in my tracks if I don't get inside soon. Steeling my resolve, I climb the three steps and push the door open. A soft bell rings above my head, and a teenager pops his head out from behind the counter.

"Hey, welcome to Brooks Books," he says, a wide grin taking over his face. His blond hair is combed back, but it's just long and unruly enough that it falls to either side in a very '90s style. He's dressed in jeans and a band tee, a nametag pinned to his chest. I smile back at him, wondering why his face is so familiar. "You're Jana, right?"

"Um, yeah…" I trail off, confused until I catch sight of his name. *Zach*. "Wait, Zach as in Wren's little brother?"

He smiles again, dimples appearing on his cheeks.

"I didn't think you'd remember me," he says, running a hand through his hair. He seems a little shy, and I can't help the grin that takes over my face. "It's been six years—I was a pimple-faced kid last time I saw you."

"You've grown up."

"I have," he nods, his blue eyes glinting. "I'm nineteen now."

"Nineteen?" *Holy shit*.

"Yeah." He moves around the counter and leans back against it, folding his arms over his chest. His biceps bulge in his t-shirt, and I blink in surprise. "Did you just get back to town?"

"Oh, uh, yeah."

"I can't imagine why you'd choose to come back," he says, glancing out the window. "I can't wait to get out of here. I got into Harvard, but I deferred a year to help Wren with Ma."

"How is your mom?" I ask, forgetting why I'm here for a minute.

"She's struggling," he says, picking at the skin near his elbow. The muscle in his jaw jumps and his Adam's apple bobs as he swallows. "Wren doesn't think she'll last the winter."

"Oh, Zach," I pause, hating the words that sit on the tip of my tongue. I'd heard them so many times in the days following my parents' deaths that I grew numb to them. They don't mean anything at all, but it's all I can offer him. "I'm so sorry."

"Thanks, Jana," he says, a sad smile on his face. He clears his throat and stands up straight. He towers over my five-foot-six frame. "So, what can I help you with today? I'm sure you didn't come into the bookshop for some lousy news about a friend."

"Oh, um, I'm actually looking for the owner," I say, unsure of myself now that I'm back on track. "I work at Little Button, and they asked me to coordinate with the owner here for the Christmas festival booth."

"Oh yeah, sure!" Zach nods, glancing at the clock. It's just after four o'clock. "Alex isn't here today, but you might catch him at Sandy's."

Of course, he owns the place.

"Sandy's?" The diner is just down the street.

"Yeah, the girls love the fries there."

Girls?

"Oh, okay. Thanks, Zach."

CHAPTER SEVEN
ALEX

With my eyes closed, I can almost picture her hazel eyes and brilliant smile, her dark blonde hair flying out behind her as she runs through the field out behind the house, sunlight flitting through the dried grass and trees. Autumn at its finest, wrapping around the woman I've loved since I met her. But then, the chilly winter air hits, tearing me from her and tossing me back into reality.

I open my eyes, focusing on the black stone block, her name the only remnant of her.

Laura May Hall
Beloved Wife and Mother
April 12, 1990-November 30, 2021

I close my eyes again, trying to pull her image back to me, trying to hold on to the memories that threaten to disappear every day without her. It's been two years since she passed, yet somehow, it feels like just yesterday. I breathe out a shuddering sigh and square my shoulders. I blink away the tears that gather in my eyes and focus on my daughters.

Maddie stands before the headstone, a Christmas poinsettia wreath clutched in her hands. Her chin quivers as she stares silently at her mother's grave, and my heart feels like it's breaking into a million little pieces.

"Okay, Maddie," I say softly. She looks up at me, Laura's hazel eyes staring back at me, piercing me to the core. "It's time."

Morgan watches from my side as Maddie steps closer to the headstone and drapes the wreath over the corner. A little sob slips past her lips, and she clings to my leg as tears pour down her ruddy cheeks. The holidays are the hardest time of year for all of us, but the girls most of all. I inhale deeply, regulating my own emotions before crouching to meet her.

"Hey, squirt," I say, pulling her into my arms in a hug. She burrows her face in my shoulder, her little arms wrapping around my neck in a vice-like grip. "Are you missing Mama?"

Her head bobs against me, and I meet Maddie's tearful eyes behind her. I struggle to find the right words to comfort my girls as the winter air whips around us, but nothing feels right. The thought of easing their pain with words of wisdom from their mother comes, but they catch in my throat.

This was never something we planned for. Laura was supposed to be here.

"I miss her, too," I say quietly. It's not what I wanted to say, but the words seem to calm the sobbing five-year-old in my arms. I swallow past the lump in my throat and lean my head against hers. "Mama loves you both very, *very* much. She will *always* love you."

"Why did Mama have to leave, Daddy?" Maddie asks, huddling beside Laura's headstone. Her words strike my heart like a bullet, opening the wound I've been fighting to keep closed for the last two years. I open my arm, and she runs into my embrace, pressing her cold nose against my neck.

"Mama wanted to stay," I say, fighting the emotions pooling in my throat and burning through me. "But she had to go to heaven."

"With baby Maddox?"

"Yes, sweetheart." I choke on the tears, almost losing the battle. I have to be strong. I clench my jaw, my eyes moving to the small plot beside my wife.

Maddox Alexander Hall
November 30, 2021

My grip on them tightens as a wave of grief washes over me, and a sob tears from me. The tears fall, and I press my face into my girls' hair to cover it. *It wasn't supposed to be this way.* I inhale, breathing in the sweet lavender scent of their shampoo as more tears pour from me. It's like a dam breaks, and I can't do anything but ride the waves as they crash over me.

The girls cling to me, their sobs evening out the longer we stay crouched together, braced against the cold. I focus on taking deep breaths, allowing my heart rate to return to normal and the tears to slow to a stop.

Once I've calmed myself, I pull back slowly. I smile gently, brushing their hair away from their tear-stained faces and placing a kiss on each of their foreheads.

"Morgan, do you want to give Maddox the wreath you brought?" I ask, picking up the small festive wreath from where she dropped it earlier. She nods, taking the decoration in her tiny hands and walking to her brother's headstone.

"Here, Maddox," she says in the softest whisper, draping it over the corner just like Maddie did. We stay there for a few more minutes, the girls speaking in soft whispers to their brother's grave while I kneel before Laura's.

I trace the letters of her name, feeling the sharp grooves cut into the stone. I close my eyes and pull her face to the surface once more, memorizing the way her lips turn up in a secret smile and how her eyes shine with excitement.

Oh, Laura. I sigh and rest my forehead against the cold stone. *I don't know how to do this on my own. Please help me give them a happy Christmas with the same love and excitement you used to instill.*

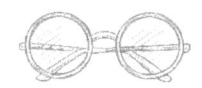

"Are you following me?" I bite out harshly, glaring at the brunette woman from the bookstore. I still have no idea what her name is, and I honestly don't care at this point. It's the third time I've run into her in the last week, and this time, it's gone too far.

We're outside Sandy's Diner, squared off to each other as the girls watch from our booth inside. The woman's eyes go wide, her smile faltering as she takes a step back in shock. I'm a little surprised by my tone as well, but I cross my arms and stand firm between her and the diner.

"No, no, not at all!" she says hurriedly. She shakes her head, knocking curls loose with the aggressiveness of the motion. "I was just looking for you—I'm Jana."

Jana. I want to say it, taste it on my tongue, but I keep it in.

"I don't care who you are," I say instead, enjoying the way her dark lashes flutter in surprise before her warm brown eyes narrow slightly. She sets her jaw, her lips pulling into a small pout as a soft *huff* escapes. *She's cute when she's angry.*

"Well, you'd better start caring," she says, folding her arms across her chest. My eyes flicker, taking in the way she holds herself. It's like she's putting on a character, trying to hide herself behind a mask of sass and attitude. *Oh, but how I would love to rip off the mask and see who she really is beneath it.*

"And why is that, *Jana*?" I can't help myself and her name rolls off my tongue. She licks her lips, and I follow the motion with rapt fascination. She swallows, her throat bobbing, and I'm enthralled by the simple act. *Shit.*

"Because we've been partnered up for the Christmas festival, *booth buddy*."

"Booth buddy?" I repeat, my throat drying up as I meet her eyes again. She's smirking, and it's the most adorable look I've ever seen. It takes a moment for her words to register and for Mayor Bradley's announcement from the town hall meeting to come back. *Little Button Bakery and Brooks Books.*

"Mrs. F is out of town for the holidays," Jana says, quirking an eyebrow. A small, smug smile pulls at her full lips, but she bites down on her bottom lip to hide it. My eyes zero in on the movement, my stomach tightening. "So, you're stuck with me."

"Stuck with you?" I want to hit myself when all I can do is repeat her words.

"I work at the bakery," she says with a shrug. "The manager put me on festival duty, so I guess we're stuck together."

I shake my head, trying to clear it. This woman is already causing chaos to unleash within me, and I can't imagine trying to work with her on something so important. The Christmas festival was Laura's favorite part of the holiday here in Harmony, and now I have to create a booth with another woman?

Jana's fingers tap absently on her arm as she scans our surroundings. "Anyway, I thought we could get together sometime and do a little brainstorming. I haven't been to a Christmas festival in Harmony in years, so I mostly just remember the games and prizes."

I clench my jaw, thinking. Maddie's ballet class was canceled at the last minute due to a flu outbreak, meaning I would be free this evening. "Why don't you come by my house? I just had some time free up."

"Oh, um..." Jana chuckles nervously as she pulls her lightweight jacket tighter around her body. "I'm actually supposed to go to Mr. Kent's tree farm with my roommate tonight."

I don't know if it's an excuse, a way to get out of going to an unknown man's house, but her words trigger a memory from a few days ago. *We are getting a tree, right, Daddy?*

"Okay, we'll come with you."

Jana's full cheeks flush a pretty pink, and I relish the reaction. "*We?*"

I smile, the first real one in days. There's something about her that makes me want to continue surprising her, to see how many times I can bring that blush to her face.

"My girls have been begging to get a tree for weeks now," I say, gesturing to the window. Maddie and Morgan are giggling uncontrollably in the booth, their chicken strips and fries forgotten on the table.

"You have kids." The surprised tone brings my gaze back to her. She stares in awe at the little girls, her brown eyes lighting up. *God, she's gorgeous.*

"It looks like they're finished," I say, startled by the intensity of my thoughts. I swallow quickly and clear my throat. "I'll pay the bill, and then we can go."

I hurry inside, away from Jana and her enticing smile and warm eyes.

CHAPTER EIGHT
JANA

The cab of this truck feels suffocating, and with every side glance he sends me, my heart beats faster. I can't think straight, especially since every deep breath I take to recenter myself is filled with the scent of cedar and orange citrus. There's an unexpected tension between us, and it takes everything in me not to break our silence. The two little girls in the backseat whisper back and forth, excited laughter filling the truck.

"Are we really getting a tree, Daddy?" the younger one pipes up finally. Alex looks at me, his jaw tight, but when he lifts his gaze to the rearview mirror, he's an entirely different person. His amber eyes soften, accompanying his lips in a smile as his entire face brightens.

"Sure are, Morgan."

Happy squeals flood the cab, and I feel an involuntary smile bloom at their delight. My eyes meet Alex's, and I bite my bottom lip to force the smile back. His expression softens, his warm amber gaze dropping to my mouth. *I'm imagining that, right? There's no way he's looking at my lips right now.* I release the hold, a soft breath sweeping from my lungs at his unexpected attention. I'm too warm, my body betraying me as it heats under his gaze.

His eyes linger a moment longer than necessary as a blush creeps up my neck and spills into my cheeks. Those golden eyes darken; whether it's a shadow crossing his face or my imagination, I'm not sure. He swallows roughly, his expression clouding as he turns away.

What is wrong *with me?* I press my palms into my thighs, hoping the pressure will ease the sudden nerves racing through me.

It doesn't help.

Alex makes a right turn onto a snowy side road that leads to the Kent's tree farm, and the girls lean forward, trying to catch a glimpse through the windshield. The farm is picture perfect, with a giant red barn and horses standing out in a paddock beside the most beautiful farmhouse. To the left is a field of evergreen trees covered in fresh snowfall.

"It's beautiful," I whisper, more to myself than anyone else. It's been years since I came to pick out a tree here, and it's more surreal than I remember. "Like it was pulled from a movie scene."

Alex parks the truck beside the gate before turning to look at his girls. His knee bumps mine, the touch lingering as he looks between his daughters, and I have to force myself not to react. It's a gentle pressure, warm and grounding, and I find my eyes drawn to where we connect.

"Alright, ladies," he says, his voice deep and gravelly. A shiver shoots up my spine, and I can't help but lift my gaze to his face. He's smiling conspiratorially with his daughters, and it does something to my insides. "We're here to get a tree, but we need to remember how big our house is. We need one just a little taller than Daddy, okay?"

The two little girls nod seriously, leaning forward to listen closely, and I grin. The older one—Maddie—looks over at me, her hazel eyes narrowing a little before she gives me a shy smile.

"What about Miss Jana's tree?" she asks. I glance at Alex, but he's already watching me. I catch my breath at the intensity behind those warm brown eyes, my cheeks flushing. I drag my gaze away from him and look between the girls, who wait for me to explain.

"Oh, my house is very small," I say. I try to pretend Alex isn't studying my side profile, but the heat from his gaze makes it difficult to focus. "I need a little tree, something a little taller than Morgan."

"That's so *tiny*!" Maddie exclaims, shock scrunching up her face.

"I am not!" Morgan whines, her brows furrowing as she pouts.

"No, you're not," I say, calming her with a sugary-sweet tone before Maddie can argue back. "It's the perfect size to go on my friend's piano."

"You have a piano?" Maddie asks, forgetting the argument she was about to make.

"Yeah." I smile, looking between the girls. They both look awestruck, but I'm confused. "Do you know how to play?"

"Daddy used to play for Mama when I was little," Maddie says with a wistful smile on her lips. I can tell I've struck a nerve when Alex tenses beside me. I peek at him out of the corner of my eye and notice the warm smile has dropped, replaced by a storm cloud of emotion. Maddie's voice is small when she speaks again, drawing my attention to the now melancholy duo in the backseat. "I miss her."

"It's okay to miss your mama," I say softly, settling my hand over hers on the back of my seat. I remember how devastated Hadlee had been when her parents separated, and she'd been older than these two. I can't imagine how difficult a divorce would be for them. My heart hammers in my chest, and I smile gently when she looks up at me through watery lashes. "I miss my mama, too."

"Where's your mama?" Morgan asks in a soft voice. I turn my attention to her, taking in her soft, wispy blonde hair and amber eyes—eyes exactly like her dad's. Her bottom lip wobbles, and I offer a kind smile, my heart hurting. It's not easy, talking about someone you lost who was so important to you, but I can't stop now.

"In heaven, I think," I say, tilting my head in thought. In truth, I'd never really thought about *where* my parents were now, simply that they were *gone*, and I couldn't get them back. Morgan's eyes widen, a delighted grin overtaking her previously saddened expression.

"Do you think your mama knows my mama?"

My heart shatters at her words, my lips parting in shock as I turn my wide eyes to Alex. His warm amber eyes have misted over, and he rubs a hand over his jaw, as if that will hold the emotions threatening to bubble over at bay. I lick my lips, swallowing past the lump forming in my throat at this new information. *Not divorced—widowed.* I want to reach out to him, to comfort him, but I know there's nothing I can do, or say, to take away the heartache he must be living through.

I press my knee firmly against his, hoping the pressure will ease him, ground him, like it did me. Turning back to the girls, I smile warmly.

"Definitely," I say, giving a sharp nod. "I think my mama is sitting with your mama and they're probably telling each other stories."

"Mama loves stories!" Morgan giggles, blinking away the dampness in her eyes. Her chubby cheeks are tinged pink, and her pretty smile brightens the mood inside the cab. I grin back at her, grateful I prevented it from progressing past misty eyes. This was supposed to be a fun outing for these girls, and by God, I would make sure it was.

"So does my mama," I say, glancing between them with a secret smile. "You know what else she loved?"

"What?" they coo in tandem. My smile widens as I turn to Alex, including him in the secret.

"Christmas."

HADLEE
this place is killing me

> ME
> the Kent's tree farm?

no, the salon.

I got held up.

> okay...

can you get the tree by yourself?

I'll send you money

> oh, i guess?
>
> I was kinda hoping you'd be here

what, why?

it's just a tree.

I'll help you decorate it when I get home tonight.

> no, it's not that.

well then what?

> ugh, nothing

no, tell me!

> it's complicated

life's complicated, bitch

Healing with You

> it's all your fault, but i'll tell you later

fine, but it better be juicy goss

🙄

all the deets, Jay

> sure, whatever
>
> see you tonight

bye bitch

I groan, tucking my phone back into my pocket. *Dammit, Hadlee.* Of course, she couldn't get off work on time. I shake my head, exhaling a deep breath. *I'm going to make the most of this.*

I'm hyper-aware of Alex's presence just behind me, the soft crunch of his boots in the snow keeping me on edge as his daughters run off ahead of us. Talking to the girls about my mom brought up an unexpected amount of emotion, and despite his nearness, I let my mind settle on my parents. The grief isn't nearly as raw as it was before, but it settles around my heart, darkening my mood like rain clouds hiding the sun.

I let my fingers caress the branches of each tree I pass, the prickle of the pine needles centering me.

My parents loved Christmas, so much so that Mom would go all out decorating the house every year. People would come from the next town over just to see the light show at the Thomas Villa. A small smile pulls at my lips as I think about our last

Christmas together. Mom had outdone herself, the display syncing to the Nutcracker Ballet.

I dash away the tears that fall, smiling when the girls look back at us before disappearing around a large evergreen. I pause beside the tree, looking up. It's exceptionally tall, probably too tall for their house. Crossing the narrow walkway, I make my way around another tree. It's about a foot taller than my five and a half feet, with full branches and a good color. It would be a lovely Christmas tree.

"Thank you," Alex says, his voice low. I peer at him through the branches, caught off guard by his words. He's been quiet since we climbed out of the truck fifteen minutes ago, keeping to himself as we followed the girls deeper into the trees.

I smile, my heart pitter-pattering at the sincerity in his tone, and the dark cloud hanging over me disperses. I have a feeling he doesn't share his thoughts often, but when he does, it's almost always important. Tucking a curl behind my ear, I let my fingers trail over the prickly boughs between us.

"Of course," I reply softly. I chew on my thumbnail for a moment, trying to gather my thoughts. The utter heartbreak I'd seen on his face when Maddie brought up her mother spoke volumes where he couldn't. I think about the years immediately following my parents' deaths, and the ache in my chest deepens. "I'm sorry to hear about your wife. I can't imagine enduring that kind of a loss."

When his eyes meet mine, it's like I'm trapped in the golden depths of them. Grief and uncertainty swirl within the amber irises, and even deeper, something more meaningful—something so powerful that I can't catch my breath. My chest swells with the overwhelming, unspoken emotions between us, and it takes everything in me not to reach out to him. *He looks so lost, so confused.*

His lips part, and I know he's about to say something important.

"*Jana.*" The way he says my name with such tenderness makes my heart skip. Our fingers brush against each other on the branches, a soft and warm caress. "I—"

"Daddy, Daddy!"

And just like that, the spell is broken. I'm thrust back into reality, into the chilly Christmas tree farm, with a chasm between Alex and me.

Morgan and Maddie rush us, smiles stretching from ear to ear. Alex catches Morgan, swinging her up and holding her on his hip.

"Hello, darlings!" he crows, all traces of vulnerability disappearing as he grins at his children. Maddie leans into me, wrapping her arms around my middle as she rests her head against my side. My heart jumps, and I smile down at her adoringly, smoothing back her soft brown hair.

"We found the *perfect* tree, Daddy," she says, out of breath.

"You did?" he asks, looking between them, his eyes twinkling. They both nod enthusiastically, broad smiles taking over their faces. "Well, you'd better show us then!"

Maddie grabs my hand and pulls me along behind her as she hurries in the direction they came from. I laugh, her excitement rubbing off on me as we all but run through the field of trees, Morgan and Alex following close behind. The smile on my face hurts, but I can't make it disappear. True joy races through me, and for the first time this holiday season, I'm actually at ease.

They truly found the perfect tree. It stands just taller than Alex, its branches full and wide. As Mr. Kent helps Alex tie it onto his truck next to my smaller tree, I hold the girls' hands, listening to their excited chattering. For a moment, it feels unreal, and I'm overcome with the realization that this has been my dream since I was a little girl: a family to share the love of Christmas with.

Sure, they aren't my family—not really. But when Alex turns toward us, a brilliant grin etched on his face, I can't help but wish they were. His whole countenance has changed from the man I first met. While his dark hair still falls in unruly curls over his forehead and his scruffy beard hides half his face, I recognize the same unbridled excitement in his expression that I see in his daughters'.

Warmth seeps through me, goosebumps rising on my arms beneath my jacket as our eyes meet. *What the hell is happening to me?* The rawness, the *realness*, is nothing I've experienced before—not with Jon and *definitely* not with George.

"Daddy, can Miss Jana help us decorate the tree?" Maddie asks, her hazel eyes blinking up at Alex as he approaches us. My eyes widen as he looks at me, both of us surprised by her request.

"Yeah, can she, Daddy?" Morgan pleads, pouting her lips and batting her lashes at her father.

"I swear I didn't put them up to this," I say with an uncomfortable laugh, my cheeks burning with embarrassment. Alex chuckles, the sound wrapping around me and sending a rush of heat through me. I'm coming to really enjoy hearing that sound.

"Well, I suppose that's entirely up to Miss Jana," he says, and my stomach tightens as my name rolls from his tongue. It's not spoken with the same tenderness as before, but there's something about it that makes my heart rate spike. I bite my tongue, trying to settle my nerves as the three of them look at me expectantly, waiting for my response.

"I would love to help you decorate," I say, feeling slightly breathless. The girls' faces light up, and when I meet Alex's gaze again, it's all I can do to keep breathing.

What is he doing to me?

CHAPTER NINE
ALEX

I struggle to untangle the lights, listening to the laughter coming from the girls in the kitchen. Lifting my gaze from the knot of twinkle lights, I see them. Morgan sits on the kitchen island, Maddie standing on a stool beside her as Jana pours hot milk into their waiting mugs.

"Okay, now take your spoon and stir all that chocolate in really well," Jana instructs, pouring out two more mugs. The girls mimic her movement as she picks up a spoon and stirs one of the mugs thoroughly. "Good job! Now, we'll add in the marshmallows and peppermint—"

"I don't like peppermint," Maddie says, scrunching her nose in distaste.

"That's okay," Jana replies, smiling sweetly down at my daughter. "You can have some extra mallows."

Maddie's face lights up as Jana divvies out the marshmallows, making sure to give her extra. Jana's eyes lift, meeting mine, and a blush brightens her face. I'm blown away by her raw beauty, and my breath catches when she offers a sweet, shy smile.

"I want extras, too!" Morgan calls, drawing Jana's attention.

I drop my gaze back to the knot in my hands, attempting to return my focus to the task I was given. My fingers work the wires, pulling them through themselves until I have a string of untangled lights, but my mind is still on the woman standing in my kitchen. My ears are tuned into the laughter and soft chatter coming from my girls.

I was worried at first that they would rebel at the thought of a new woman coming into their lives, but Jana's presence here disproves that theory. I'm pleasantly surprised with how taken they are with her, especially Maddie.

While Morgan was three when Laura died and barely remembers her, Maddie has distinct memories of her mother, as evident in their conversation about the piano in the truck. I'm still in awe at how elegantly Jana handled such a delicate topic and Maddie's responding emotions.

As I turn to face the tree, my eyes land on the baby grand that sits in the corner of the room. I haven't played since Laura passed, but I can't seem to bring myself to get rid of it. So, it sits untouched, a constant reminder of days past and the love I lost.

I begin wrapping lights around branches of the tree, turning my back to the cocoa-making to put my full attention on finishing this task so they can hang ornaments. Gritting my teeth, I try to ignore the guilt seeping into my heart for bringing Jana here. This is the home I made with Laura, a sacred space that holds more memories than I can count. How can I bring another woman here?

"Can I set up the train, Daddy?" Maddie asks, suddenly beside me. I turn to see her perched on the armrest of the couch, an excitement I haven't seen in months lighting her face.

"You know that's the last step, Mads," I say with a laugh, tucking the memories and guilt behind a wall of stone. I continue lacing the lights around the tree, branch after branch. "But you and Morgan can set it up together when we finish decorating the tree."

"But Morgan doesn't even like trains," Maddie pouts, glaring at her sister who sits on the couch with her mug of cocoa.

"I like trains," Morgan says, but her attention is on counting her marshmallows.

"Trains are fun," Jana says, her voice surprisingly close behind me. I turn, startling her, and she stumbles back a step, her eyes going wide as hot chocolate sloshes up the sides of the mugs she's holding. Without much thought, my arm shoots around her waist, holding her upright with the cocoa between us.

Her breathing is heavy, and I try not to focus on the rise and fall of her full chest. She swallows roughly and licks her lips as she checks to make sure the drinks didn't spill. I stare at her mouth, wondering if those plump pink lips are as soft as they look.

"I'm sorry," she says, blinking up at me. I can't drag my gaze from her lips; all I want to do is lean in and claim them with mine, kissing her until neither of us can breathe. "I didn't mean to startle you. I, uh...I made you hot chocolate."

"Thank you," I say softly, dragging my eyes to hers. The dark color isn't solid like I initially thought, and standing this close, I can see the starburst of gold at the center branching out and spreading like stardust. Her lashes are long and dark, and the splattering of freckles across her face acts almost like a mask around those beautiful eyes.

"Daddy, can I put the angel on top?" Morgan asks, shattering the tension. I take the mug from Jana, my eyes dropping to her lips one more time before I turn away. Mentally shaking myself, I take a small sip of the hot chocolate and fight to get my wits about me. It tastes sweet, a rich chocolate with just a hint of peppermint.

"Sure, baby," I reply absentmindedly to Morgan. My heart is pounding in my ears, and I'm uncomfortably aware of Jana's every move. She moves to sit beside Morgan on the couch, perching on the edge with her mug clasped between her hands.

"Daddy, do you think Santa will bring me a train?" Maddie asks, and I tear my gaze from Jana. Maddie has draped herself across the armrest, her feet up and crossed at the ankles. They all watch me as I move back to the tree, setting my mug on the coffee table before continuing with the lights.

"What kind of train?" Jana asks, and I chuckle, shaking my head. *Oh, she's started it now.*

"I really want a steam engine," Maddie says. "Lionel has a really cool model that's electric—it blows steam and everything. I just haven't saved up enough to get one yet."

"Lionel?"

"Oh, that's the company that makes model trains."

"Oh." Jana's surprise is audible. "You know a lot about trains then?"

"A lot? She's practically an encyclopedia for trains, aren't you, Mads?" I laugh softly, glancing briefly at my oldest daughter. Her cheeks are flushed, her hazel eyes downcast as she fiddles with a loose string on the arm she's spread out on. Regret washes through me when I see her disappointment. *I can never do anything right with her.*

"Really?" Jana asks. Maddie nods but bites her lip in embarrassment. "What's your favorite train?"

Maddie looks up, hope in her gaze as she studies the woman. I study her as well, surprised at her interest. Nobody ever appreciates Maddie's love of trains; their eyes typically glazing over within minutes of bringing it up. "Steam trains or freight trains?"

"Oh, um..." Jana pauses, her eyes darting to me as a confused expression clouds her beautiful face. She bites her thumbnail, a habit of hers I've noticed is linked to nerves. "What about both?"

"Well, my favorite steam engine is the Flying Scotsman," Maddie says, tilting her head in thought. "That's the one they used in the *Harry Potter* movies. But my favorite freight train is the Santa Fe freight because it can tow 180 tons—do you know how much that is?"

I've made it around to the other side of the tree and can see both of them clearly now. Maddie's face has lit up, and it warms my heart. I watch Jana for a moment, her eyes glued to my older daughter as she strokes Morgan's hair where she lays in her lap, her cocoa forgotten. She's giving Maddie her full attention, something I've struggled to do consistently over the last two years.

"How much?" she asks.

"Three hundred and sixty *thousand* pounds."

"Wow, that's a lot!" Jana exclaims, bringing a smile to my face.

"I know!" Maddie sits up, swinging her legs around to rest on the couch cushion as she stares at Jana in delight. "Did you know the oldest running train is called *The Fairy Queen*? Isn't that so *dreamy*? *The Fairy Queen*—it sounds like something from a storybook."

"*Maddie*," I warn gently, glancing at Jana. I don't want Maddie's fascination with trains to annoy her, the way most people become annoyed. "Why don't we start decorating now?"

Maddie's shoulders slump, and I sigh softly. *Dammit, I did it again.* Jana's gaze locks with mine, concern racing across her face. I'm not sure what she sees in my expression, but concern is quickly replaced by understanding and a small, sweet smile.

"Oh, I don't mind," she says, turning back to my daughter and offering a wide grin. Maddie's face lights up, but she reaches to open a box of ornaments anyway. "How old is *The Fairy Queen*, Maddie?"

"It was built in 1855," Maddie says, walking toward the tree. Pushing up on her tiptoes, she reaches as high as she can to place the little glass ornament on a branch. "That's 168 years old. It's in India. Did you know it's got the world record for being the oldest running train?"

"That's impressive," Jana says, helping Morgan stand and get her own ornament. I watch them as I finish the lights, my heart full. "You know, I used to ride a train *every day* when I was in college. It was my favorite part of the day."

"Really?" If possible, Maddie's eyes widen even more. "That would be so cool!"

"It was," Jana whispers back, hanging up her own ornament. Our eyes lock through the tree branches, and my heartbeat skyrockets at the secret smile she sends me. I feel like a kid with a crush, my palms sweating as I step around the tree.

"Daddy, can we go on a train ride, too?" Maddie asks, turning to me as I get closer.

"I don't know if there are any trains around here," I say, coming to a stop beside Jana. She looks up through her lashes, holding an ornament out to me. Her shyness is adorable, yet so different from how she interacts with my girls. I smile as I take the bauble, our fingers brushing as I do. An electric shock shoots from her hand to mine, and our eyes lock.

"I'm sorry," she says breathlessly, her tongue swiping out and drawing my gaze to those goddamn pillow lips. It's all too tempting to lean down and claim her mouth, but I can't. Standing this close to her, watching her dark lashes flutter against the gentle swell of her cheeks, and inhaling that tempting honey-cinnamon scent that surrounds her, it's hard to remember that. *I can't do this—I can't kiss her.*

"No worries," I reply, taking a step back. I turn to hang the ornament, trying to collect myself before I do something stupid—like fall head-over-heels for this girl.

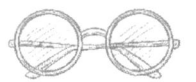

Wren arrives to watch the girls around eight so I can take Jana home. Three sharp knocks sound on the front door, and I open it to find the blonde, looking more tired than usual. Her mismatched green and blue eyes shine with unshed tears, her hair piled on top of her head in a messy bun.

"Hey, Alex," she says softly, stepping inside.

"Hey, are you good?" I ask, closing the door behind her. She chuckles wryly but nods, her eyes darting to the brunette in the living room.

"Jana?"

Jana turns from where she was draping a blanket over a sleeping Morgan, surprise lighting up her face. "Wren, hi!"

"What are you doing here?" my babysitter asks, meeting Jana halfway and giving her a big hug. Surprise floods through me at the instant recognition between them. I mean, sure, Harmony is a small town, but they seem to know each other better than that. "I thought Hadlee was taking you tree shopping tonight."

"Oh, she got held up at the salon," Jana says, her cheeks tinging red as her eyes dart to me. "And Alex needed to get one as well, so he offered to go with me."

I can't see Wren's face, but the way Jana's cheeks flush a deeper red, I'm sure there's something unspoken between the two. I busy myself, grabbing a flannel to toss over the t-shirt I'm wearing and trying to ignore the glances sent my way. My phone rings as I tug the flannel up my arms. Pulling it out, I glance at the screen. *Leslie*.

"I hope you had fun," Wren whispers, and I lift my gaze to them. Wren gives Jana another hug, tighter this time. I ignore the call, tucking the phone back into my pocket. "And I want to hear everything tomorrow."

I smirk, enjoying the way Jana's cheeks deepen to a shade of red I haven't seen before. She waves the blonde off with a laugh before saying her goodbyes. She walks toward me, biting her bottom lip and avoiding my eyes as I open the door for her. I let her walk a little ahead of me, and by the time we reach my truck, her blush has faded to a soft flush.

I open her door, offering her a hand to climb inside the cab. Our fingers brush lightly before the touch solidifies into a tight grip. Her skin is soft on mine, and I can feel the rush of her pulse beneath my fingertips at her wrist.

My own heart seems to be racing, and as she looks up at me with those wide brown eyes, I almost give in to my body's basest desire. *I want to kiss her—no, I need to kiss her.* Her warm, soft body is so close, I can almost imagine how she would fit against me. I can feel her breath on my face, her lips parting in shock as I lean closer, the urge to claim her mouth growing every second we stand there.

"*Alex...*" Her lashes flutter, her face tilting toward me, and I feel myself giving in. *What's the harm if I did?* Lifting a hand, I brush her dark curls, so different from Laura's blonde, away from her cheek. *Laura.* As my fingers brush against her soft skin, a sharp pain shoots through my chest at the reminder of my wife.

That's the harm. How could I betray Laura this way?

I stumble back, dropping my hand like I've been burned by hot coals. I let my attraction to Jana get out of hand, allowing my urges to run the show—but no more. I need to cool it, let these conflicting emotions settle before making any more decisions.

I avoid Jana's confused gaze as I wordlessly help her into the truck before slamming the door shut and walking around to the driver's side. I climb in and start the engine, backing out without another glance her way.

The drive to her house is all too quiet, filled with the low hum of the radio. It's only a ten-minute drive, but in the tense silence, it feels longer. I can feel Jana's eyes on me throughout the drive, but I do my best to ignore it. My feelings are warring beneath the surface, and I keep my face emotionless the whole time.

I've loved Laura since I met her. We were college sweethearts, and I knew the moment I saw her that I would marry her. Our love story wasn't one you would read in a fairytale, but it was perfect to me. We were married for eight years before I lost her due to complications during birth. Maybe it would've been easier had Maddox lived, but his life ended within hours of hers.

I never thought I would find someone to love the way I did Laura. She had my whole heart and soul—yet the intense feelings I felt throughout the day were far too real for me. Jana is effortlessly beautiful and kind, with a gentle yet incredibly strong presence. She knows who she is and never strays from it; a trait I value and know my girls need in their lives.

Pulling up in front of the small white house she directs me to, I shift into park and wait for a moment, trying to gather my thoughts. Jana clicks open her seatbelt and grabs her bag from the seat beside her.

"Thanks for the ride," she says, her voice barely above a whisper and full of an emotion I'm terrified to analyze. I nod, not trusting myself to speak, or even move. I keep my hands firmly on the steering wheel, my eyes locked on the large pine tree at the end of the street. "I suppose we can schedule another time to plan for the booth."

Again, I nod.

"Can I, um..." Her words trail off with a nervous laugh, and I can't help myself. I turn to look at her. I clench my jaw, wishing I could see the pretty pink blush that's sure to be staining her cheeks. Her eyes are downcast, her teeth gripping tightly at her full bottom lip in a way that begs me to release it. My hands tighten on the steering wheel, my palms damp with sweat. *I swear to God...* "I thought maybe we should, um...maybe we should exchange numbers?"

That's when I notice she's holding her phone out to me.

I hold out my hand, and she sets it in my palm with a fleeting brush of fingertips that ignites a fire under my skin. I swallow roughly past the lump forming in my throat and quickly type my number into a new contact. I send myself a text before I can convince myself it's a bad idea. It's almost too tempting, knowing I can message her at any time. I grit my teeth and hand the phone back to her.

This time, our fingers linger, and heat spreads from the touch.

I meet her gaze, and everything in me screams to gather her in my arms and kiss her senseless. I'm oddly aware of my heart thumping in my chest, and it pains me to pull away. Jana looks away, disappointment clear on her face despite her attempt to hide it. My chest tightens with anger at myself. I want to comfort her, but the lingering sting of betrayal haunts me. Laura is my wife, the only woman I've ever loved, the one I vowed to love for eternity.

"Okay, I'll text you then," Jana says, opening her door. The cab light turns on, and I can finally see her face clearly once more. *I was right.* Her cheeks are stained pink. She bites her bottom lip again, and it's all I can do not to reach over and release it with my thumb. *If she keeps doing that...*

"Yeah, sounds good," I say with a nod.

She smiles, a sweet, melancholy smile that doesn't quite reach her eyes. "Bye, Alex."

"Goodbye, Jana."

CHAPTER TEN
JANA

"So, wait a minute." Hadlee shakes her head, pressing a freshly manicured nail against her temple. She studies me from across the table. "Are you still sworn off guys? Or did we forgo that entirely when you found out the bookworm is actually a sweet single dad?"

I bite a little too deeply into my cuticle and wince at the pain that blossoms. It's been two days since I went to the tree farm with Alex and his daughters; two days since the most confusing night of my life. I've avoided texting him to set up a brainstorming session, too embarrassed by the unexpected rejection. I mean, I hadn't even remembered to collect the damn Christmas tree from the bed of his truck.

"I don't know," I say, tucking my hands under my thighs. My anxiety has been off the charts since that night with Alex, and my poor cuticles have taken the brunt of the emotions. "One minute, he was a total dick, and then suddenly, he's this sweet, understanding, *widowed* father with a smile that could give you a fucking heart attack. I just...I don't know how I feel."

"Do you think he's just guarded?" Quinn asks, picking at the fries in front of her. "From what Wren's told me about him, it would make total sense."

"Yeah." Hadlee nods along, swirling the straw in her milkshake. "Maybe he's just protecting his heart, and in turn his daughters', by putting up this *tough guy* exterior."

"You think so?" I ask, leaning forward a little and resting my arms on the table. I pick up a fry, thinking about the other night. "I dunno. I mean, I *swear* he was going to kiss me, and then it was like he'd been burned, and I got the cold shoulder the whole drive home."

My heart had about burst through my chest when he leaned so close that I could smell the peppermint cocoa on his breath. And feeling his touch on my cheek—I'd almost melted right into the snow. Despite our short time together, I'd been ready and *willing* for that kiss to happen. His complete 180 bruised my ego.

"Maybe he's concerned his daughters will see him dating someone new as him trying to replace their mom," Hadlee suggests. I raise my eyebrows, and she shrugs, meeting my eyes with a half-smile. "My parents got divorced, remember? When my dad got remarried, I was so mad that he'd replaced my mom so quickly—so easily."

It makes sense. With the way Maddie spoke about her mother with the utmost reverence, I could see why Alex might be worried about that. I shake my head. "But I don't want to replace their mom."

"That won't matter to them." Hadlee smiles sympathetically. "All they're gonna see is their dad smitten by a new woman and forgetting about their mom."

The thought of Alex being smitten by *me* is enough to make my cheeks heat. I glance between my friends, both studying me with piercing gazes.

"I don't even want to date Alex," I say, crossing my arms. My fingers tap a rhythm out on my arm as anxiety begins to creep in. Sure, I'm attracted to him—more than I've been to any other guy I've met before—but that doesn't mean anything. Not really. Attraction is only one piece of the puzzle, and it's not even the most important part.

"Are you sure?" Quinn asks, popping a fry into her mouth. She smiles while she chews, and I shake my head. "Your blush begs to differ."

"I told you—I'm done with men." Even if he's the kindest, most attractive man I've met.

"But that was before," Hadlee points out. She sips on her milkshake, a small smile in her eyes.

"Where's Wren?" I ask, changing the subject. I need to stop talking about Alex before I start analyzing the looks and touches we'd shared. "I thought she was meeting us here."

"She'll be here," Quinn says, glancing at her phone. "She just had to pick up her mom's meds from the pharmacy."

"How's Heidi doing?" Hadlee asks, finally dragging that scrutinizing gaze from me. Quinn shrugs, playing with the end of her ponytail.

"Wren doesn't really talk about it," she says, concern leaking into her voice and expression. "But I'm pretty sure it's not good."

"I saw Zach at the bookstore the other day," I say, remembering my conversation with our friend's little brother. "He said they're not sure she'll make it through the year."

"Poor Wren," Hadlee says softly. We grow silent, and a gnawing sadness takes root in my chest. Losing a parent is one of the hardest things a person can go through. Mine died unexpectedly, a horrible car accident taking them from me and my sister before their time. I can't even imagine what Wren must be going through, watching her mother lose her mind as she slowly loses her life.

"Let's talk about something else," Quinn says, her attention on something outside. "She just got out of her car."

"Like what?" Hadlee side-eyes the redhead as she drums her nails on the linoleum tabletop. "Our plans for Christmas?"

"Sure, why not?"

"Her mama might not live through the holiday, Q," Hadlee scoffs, smoothing her glossy black hair with one hand. She eats another fry, glancing at the door. "Do you really think she'll wanna talk about those plans?"

"Well, I think we should do our best to raise her spirits."

"I agree, but I don't think Christmas plans are the way to do that."

I listen to my friends bicker as I stare off into space. Talk of loss and death brings a heaviness to my chest I can't seem to shake, even in the company of loved ones. While my parents' deaths had been years ago, the memory of them lingers. Grief can be painful, but mostly it's become a deep, achy sadness anytime I think of them.

"Wren! You made it!" Quinn's words shake me out of my stupor, and I screw a smile onto my face. Wren doesn't need my melancholy to add to her plate. Besides, this is supposed to be a nice lunch with friends.

"Sorry I'm late," Wren says, sliding into the booth beside me and shrugging off her coat. She lifts a hand, getting the waitress's attention. "I forgot to get Mama's new meds refilled. What did I miss?"

"We were just talking about Alex Hall and his hot and cold treatment of Jana," Hadlee says, lifting a fry to her lips as Wren orders a lemonade and a chicken salad. I glare at my best friend, hating that the conversation has been brought back around to the confusing situationship that is Alex and me.

"Oh, he's really a nice guy, Jana, I promise," Wren says, turning to face me with wide, mismatched eyes. "That family has just had it rough the last few years."

"Yeah, I heard about his wife," I say, tucking stray curls behind my ear. Learning about his loss had made a lot of things click into place in my mind, but it didn't make anything any less confusing—or complicated. "I can't really blame him—loss does something to you. It's just extremely confusing, that's all."

"Just give him time," she says, smiling softly. "The Hall men are broody, but all they need is a little time to work through their feelings."

"How is Benji, anyway?" Hadlee asks with a smirk. Wren's cheeks turn a soft shade of pink, but she simply rolls her eyes.

"I don't know. I'm not his keeper," she says, leaning back in the booth. "Besides, I've been kinda busy lately. I haven't seen him much."

"That's odd," Quinn quips, joining Hadlee in her teasing. "You two seem to be joined at the hip most days."

"You guys are so off base," Wren says with a laugh. "Benji and I are just friends."

"*Right.*"

ALEX
When do you want to get together?

Healing with You

I hold my breath, my chest tightening in anticipation. The text came hours after I left the girls at the table, the conversation still stupidly fresh in my mind. *Just give him time.* I shake my head and release a laugh. *I don't even want to date right now!* I run a hand through my hair and breathe out slowly.

ALEX
to brainstorm, I mean.

Right. The festival is quickly approaching, and we still haven't decided what our booth will be.

ME
you could come over tonight

around 6?

ALEX
I'll need to bring the girls.

that's fine, they're the sweetest

That's definitely a word for it.

Are you sure we'll be able to get work done?

of course!

we can bake cookies and then they can watch a movie while we talk

I'm sure they'd love that.

I chew on my bottom lip, wondering how exactly I'm going to survive a night with those soulful eyes and full, kissable lips. I shake my head again, trying to shake those thoughts from my head. Hadlee would be there, and so would the girls.

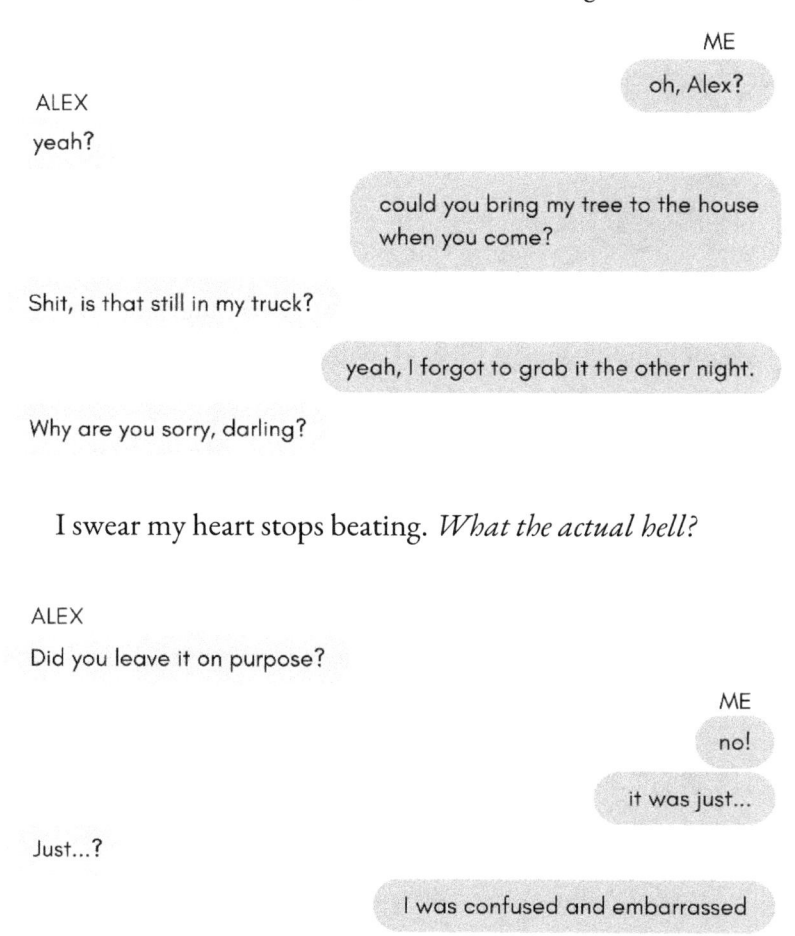

> **ME**
> oh, Alex?

ALEX
yeah?

> could you bring my tree to the house when you come?

Shit, is that still in my truck?

> yeah, I forgot to grab it the other night.

Why are you sorry, darling?

I swear my heart stops beating. *What the actual hell?*

ALEX
Did you leave it on purpose?

> **ME**
> no!
>
> it was just...

Just...?

> I was confused and embarrassed

I can't believe I actually sent that message. I stare at my phone, watching the three little dots appear and disappear as he types. Anxiety begins building, and I feel my chest tighten. Breathing is harder when my anxiety acts up, and I close my eyes in an attempt to calm myself as I deepen my shallow breaths. The soft *ding* of an incoming text brings me back.

> **ALEX**
> I'm so sorry, Jana.

I stare in shock as the words register in my mind. *He's sorry.*

> **ALEX**
> I'm sorry for being an absolute dick when we first met. You just caught me so off guard and I took my anger out on you. I hope you can forgive me.

It's a no-brainer for me, and as I type out the response, I feel my anxiety fleeing.

> **ME**
> of course I forgive you

Even spending a day with him, I could tell his reaction that first day was just that—a reaction. He's not that guy. He's sweet and kind, and strong and...and he's Alex.

I sigh, rubbing a hand over my eyes. Despite everything I've told my friends, everything I continue to tell *myself*, some part of me cares. It's the same part that screams at me for holding back, for not taking what I wanted that night and kissing him.

> **ALEX**
> I'll see you tonight, darling.

My heart jumps, and I roll over, screaming into the pillow. *What the hell is happening?*

CHAPTER ELEVEN
JANA

I peer at myself in the bathroom mirror and run a hand over the unruly mane of mismatched curls. I know there's not much I can do to tame them, except for maybe tying them up, but that would defeat the purpose. I spent far too long in the bathroom with the diffuser to simply tie my hair up in my usual messy bun.

I feel silly, having spent so long on my appearance, but as my stomach tightens in anticipation, I swipe bright red lipstick over my lips. Alex and the girls would be here any minute. I flop my hair the opposite way and glare hard at my reflection. My heart is pounding in my chest, and nothing I do can make it stop.

I shake my head and rub the lipstick off with a wipe. It smears a little, and I groan, rubbing at the stain. I never wear makeup, and this is the worst time to try it out.

"They're here!" Hadlee calls from the living room.

I toss the wipe in the trashcan and take one last glance at my reflection. The lipstick is mostly gone, leaving a light stain of pink I really can't fix now. I tug at the hem of my oversized sweater—the only Christmas sweater I keep. It's red, the same shade as the lipstick I so foolishly tried to wear. The design is simple, and I can't help but smile when I look at it. White snowflakes are woven over the entire thing, while a reindeer sits at the center, lights tangled in his antlers.

My mother gave me this sweater before I left for college, a few months before the car accident. It's the only piece of her I have left, and I love it. I smile softly at my reflection before leaving the bathroom.

As I leave my room, there's a soft knock on the front door.

Hadlee glances at me from the couch where she's reading a romance novel, and I glare playfully at her. "What? I heard his truck pull up."

"Remember, best behavior, Lee," I say, ruffling my curls as I make my way across the house. It's a wide-open floor plan, meaning I can see the kitchen from my bed if my door is open. Hadlee hasn't bought a dining room table, so there's a wide-open space between the front door and the back of the couch she's perched on.

Hadlee smirks as I walk past her, her green eyes sparkling with mischief. "I'm always on my best behavior."

"Okay," I smile and roll my eyes. "Be on *my* best behavior, then."

Her laugh follows me to the door. The tension leaves my shoulders as my best friend's playfulness eases my anxiety. This is why we're such a good pair—she's the Dean to my Sam, and I wouldn't trade it for anything.

I pause when my fingers close over the doorknob and take a deep breath before pulling it open. Maddie and Morgan beam up at me, their smiles infectious.

"Miss Jana!"

"Hello, darlings!" I coo, unable to control myself. They rush me, and I open my arms to welcome them. Their little bodies are warm, and I squeeze them tightly in a hug. Spending all those hours with them, I've become quite attached. *I missed them.* The girls pull away, and I hold them at arm's length, taking in their appearance. Maddie wears a black leotard and pink tights under her winter coat, her hair tied in a messy ballerina bun, while Morgan sports a pretty pink dress. "Oh my! You two look lovely tonight."

"I had ballet," Maddie says matter-of-factly, shrugging off her coat. I smile, watching her step around me and kick off her winter boots.

Morgan tugs at my sleeve, and I turn my attention back to her. She holds her coat out to the side and spins in a circle. The skirt of her dress flares out, and she looks like a pretty little flower. When she comes to a stop, she grins at me. "Daddy took me to Sandy's for dinner."

Everything in me screams to find Alex's eyes at the mention of him, but I force myself to keep my attention on the grinning five-year-old. "Did you have a fun time?"

"Yes, I got fries and chicken and, and a..." She trails off, looking up at her dad, who hovers right behind her.

I finally lift my gaze, and my heart skips a beat. Alex had clearly shaved recently, his beard no longer a scruffy mess, but a neatly trimmed shadow that accentuates his sharp jaw even more. He wears a plaid flannel shirt over his usual t-shirt and jeans. My small tree is hefted over his shoulder as he stands in the doorway, waiting patiently as ever for us to finish our conversation.

"A milkshake, bug." His gravelly voice traces down my spine, leaving goosebumps to spread over my skin.

"Alex, hi." My voice is breathless, and the way he's watching me has my heart pounding against my ribs. I stand, pulling Morgan to the side to allow him inside before I close the door.

"Hello, darling." Those amber-brown eyes never leave mine, and suddenly, I feel way too warm in this sweater. *Darling.* I think I might actually pass out from how fast my heart is beating. "Where do you want this?"

He lifts the shoulder propping the tree up, and my eyes drag to the hand holding the trunk.

"Oh, um..." I trail off and bite my bottom lip, dazed by his mere presence. *Has he always been that tall?* It feels like he towers over me, despite our mere four- or five-inch height difference. I swallow and turn my attention back to his face. There's a small, amused smile pulling at his lips, and I can't even remember the question he asked me.

"You can bring the tree over here," Hadlee says, jumping in to save me when she realizes I'm not going to answer anytime soon. Alex nods, his eyes flickering over my face before he drags his gaze to my friend on the couch. "I'm Hadlee, Jana's best friend."

"Alex," he says gruffly, his eyes darting back to mine. He steps around me after a moment, walking toward Hadlee.

"Thanks for bringing the tree over, *Alex*." Hadlee stands, crossing her arms over her chest as Alex brushes past her. He sets the tree down beside the couch, and Hadlee strolls over to his side. "It is *so* unlike Jana to forget something so large and...important."

I glare at her when she looks my way with a smirk, but she simply laughs. I should've known she would tease me the whole damn time.

Maddie and Morgan each grab one of my hands, pulling me after their father.

"Why don't you help Jana set this up on the piano?" Hadlee says, leaning her hip against the side of the baby grand. It was a gift from her father when she graduated from college with a music minor. We still laugh about the fact that she went into cosmetology afterward. She waggles her fingers in a wave to the girls, grinning mischievously. "The girls and I can start on the cookie dough."

"You'll start on the cookie dough?" I ask, raising my eyebrows as Morgan hops excitedly from one foot to the other. Hadlee hasn't baked a thing since we were in high school, and she almost burned down the economics classroom.

"It's not that hard to follow a recipe, Jay." The teasing glint in her eyes belies the pout she wears, and I shake my head. "I won't burn down the kitchen, if that's what you're worried about. We're just gonna mix some ingredients together. Isn't that right, ladies?"

Maddie and Morgan nod enthusiastically, grins plastered from ear to ear.

"Do you have a pot or something you want it in?" Alex asks, sufficiently shutting down any potential arguments. Hadlee and I both swing our eyes to him. He hovers beside the tree, his hands shoved into his jean's pockets and an amused glint in his eyes.

"Yeah, there should be one in the garage," Hadlee says, pointing to the door on the other side of the room. Alex nods and moves toward it as Hadlee strides to my side. Maddie and Morgan release my hands, taking off to explore the kitchen. Their giggles fill the house, warming my heart even more. Hadlee nudges my arm with a sharp elbow, and I shoot her a questioning glance. Alex disappears into the garage, and she grins playfully. "You did *not* tell me he was that hot."

"*Hadlee.*" A warning.

"What?" she asks, letting her eyes dart to where Alex disappeared before turning her attention back to me. "All I'm saying is, I would let him be *my* daddy any day."

"Oh my God." I'm absolutely mortified, my cheeks heating in a hot blush. "I said best behavior, Lee."

The smile she sends me is devious. "Oh, I know."

"I can get this potted if you two want to start on those cookies with Maddie and Morg." His voice sends a shiver down my spine, much closer than he should be. *What if he heard Hadlee's comment?* My stomach drops. His tone is soft, barely a whisper when he says, "And then we can start that brainstorming you mentioned."

My mouth dries, the blush sliding down my neck and chest, heating my entire body. *Oh, he definitely heard.*

"Sounds good, Pops," Hadlee says with a smirk. I grab her arm, mortification keeping me from turning to face the handsome man behind me. I don't know how I'll face him now, or ever again. I hear his deep chuckle, a sound that causes butterflies to erupt in my gut and try to fight the urge growing inside me to fall at his feet.

"You've got to stop it, Lee," I whisper as we move into the kitchen. I know it's an impossible task for her—that's just who she is.

"You know I love you, Jay," she says, tying her sleek hair up into a messy bun. She grins, pulling out a bowl. "I'll behave, I promise."

I don't know if I believe you.

Forty-five minutes later, Maddie slides the first tray of sugar cookies into the oven. Morgan and Hadlee sit beside each other on the floor in front of the TV, debating which Christmas movie to watch.

I wipe my arm across my forehead, overheating and slightly overwhelmed. Baking with kids is harder than I realized. It took us two tries to make the dough, then three tries to get it rolled out and cut into the shapes they wanted.

"Good job, Maddie," I say as she closes the oven. I set my little kitchen timer and show it to her. "Ten minutes, and then we can get them out. Why don't you go watch a movie with Morgan and Hadlee while your dad and I talk?"

"Okay, Miss Jana," she says, a wide smile on her face. I watch her run into the living room, a smile pulling at my lips. Even if it was overwhelming and took twice as long as normal, I'm glad we did it. I love seeing that smile on her little face. I've grown attached to Maddie and Morgan. Losing the relationship I'm building with them would be heartbreaking.

"You're good with her," Alex says, coming up behind me. I can feel his warmth against my back, and I have to remind myself not to lean into him. It would be so easy to rest against him, let him hold me as I watched the girls play with Hadlee. *But that's not my place.*

I turn around, tilting my chin up to meet his dark gaze. His cedar and orange cologne floods my senses, and this close, I can see every single eyelash framing those captivating amber eyes.

"It's easy with her," I reply, offering a smile. My fingers tighten around the dish towel in my hands. "She knows what she wants and what she likes, and she's not ashamed of it. She's absolutely amazing, Alex. You've done a brilliant job raising her—raising both of them, really."

"Thank you, Jana," he says softly, his lips tilting up. I follow the movement in rapt attention. His lips are full and surrounded by short scruffy hairs, and I wonder what it would feel like to have the softness of his lips against mine, the rough hairs creating friction between us. I swallow roughly, mentally shaking myself. *Not the time to fantasize, Jana.* The smile on his lips grows. "Should we start, then?"

I blink, lifting my gaze back to his. He waits patiently for my response, his smile morphing into a smirk the longer it takes me to respond. "Start?"

"Brainstorming?" he says, amusement in his tone. I shake my head and squeeze my eyes shut, feeling like an idiot.

"Brainstorming, right!" I laugh nervously. "Let's do it. Do you have any thoughts?"

"I think it's important to include elements of both the bakery and the bookshop," Alex says, walking around the kitchen island.

"I agree." I follow him around and perch on the stool beside him. He opens a notebook I hadn't noticed before, and I scan the color-coded notes. My arm brushes his, and I pull back quickly. Heat blooms from where we touched, and when I lift my gaze to his, he's already watching me. I blink, surprised to see a pair of round, wire-frame glasses perched on his nose. "Uhm, wh-what do you think of a prize wheel?"

"Spin the wheel, get a prize—that sort of thing?"

"Yeah, only instead of candy, you get treats from the bakery," I say, nodding as more ideas come to mind. I push away the awkwardness that comes any time I'm around him and focus on the task at hand. "We could get specialty bookmarks and pens, too."

"Would we have anything else at the booth, or just the wheel?" Alex asks, his hand moving across the page. I nibble on the cuticle of my thumb, thinking again.

"We can sell our goods." I lean my head on my free hand, watching him. His dark hair flops over his forehead and into his eyes, his lips moving slowly as he scribbles into the notebook. "Like, um...gingerbread cookies? Or apple pies, maybe."

"I love apple pie," he says offhandedly. His eyes skim the page. "How about the bookstore?"

"Oh, um...you could do something with books..." I trail off, trying to think. It's kind of difficult when he presses the end of his pen between his lips. His teeth scrape across the click-top, and a shiver runs down my spine. "Oh...what about those "Blind Date with a Book" things?"

"What is that?" He looks up at me, curiosity written in his raised eyebrow and quirked lips. I laugh, drumming my fingers on the counter. Apparently, that's a trend that hasn't hit this small town yet.

"Exactly what it sounds like," I reply, tilting my head to look at what he's written, but I can't decipher it. His handwriting is little more than chicken scratch. I turn back to him and smile. "You wrap a book and write the very basics on it. Say it's a locked-door mystery thriller—you write that down with a very basic summary of the story so the person doesn't know what book it is and can't judge based on the cover or anything. It's a fun way to explore new books."

"Oh, that's brilliant, Jana." His grin is wide and infectious. I can't keep my smile from growing, even as a blush heats my cheeks and butterflies erupt in my tummy. I bite my bottom lip in an effort to tame the pleased grin, but that only draws his attention to my mouth. I watch his Adam's apple bob as he swallows, his eyes flickering up to mine after lingering a moment too long. "Would you want to help me choose some books for this "Blind Date" thing?"

"I'd be happy to, Alex."

CHAPTER TWELVE
ALEX

The bookshop is quiet, the girls' laughter echoing from the back of the store to mingle with Benji's droning voice. I stare absently at the screen in front of me, his words flowing in one ear and out the other, and I can't help but frown at the direction my thoughts seem to be going. Christmas is creeping closer, the festival even more so. Knowing my time with Jana is coming to an end feels like a rock sitting on my chest.

Ever since she walked into my shop it feels like we've been pushed together, and pretty soon, we won't have any external forces drawing us together. The rock grows heavier at the thought. Despite my reservations, Jana has become an important person in my daughters' lives—in *my* life—and I can't imagine losing the fragile connection we've made.

"Are you listening, Alex?" Benji's voice suddenly seems louder, and the numbers on the screen blare to life. I rub my eyes, setting my reading glasses on the counter.

"Of course, I'm listening, Benji." I had been listening—until my mind wandered from the numbers to those gorgeous chocolate brown eyes. It's like she's taken over every thought in my head, and I can't get her out.

"Where is your head, brother?" he asks, turning to face me. He folds his arms, leaning against the counter to wait me out. "You've been distracted all week."

"Don't be silly. Everything's good."

Everything, except that my feelings for Jana have become so overwhelming, to the point I can barely contain them. The rock sinks deeper, my chest aching. Loving Laura had been easier than breathing; that's how I knew she was the one. How is it possible to have found another beautiful woman who could draw out my love faster than the beat of my heart?

"You're the worst liar I've ever met, Alex."

I shake my head, chuckling lightly. "And you're so great at it?"

"I never said that," he says, ruffling his hair. Harper whines at his feet, staring up at him with big blue eyes full of concern. She sits up, leaning against his leg to offer a counterweight. Benji shifts imperceptibly, and had I not been watching so closely, I wouldn't have seen the slight pinch in his expression.

"Is your leg bugging you?" I ask, bracing a hand on his arm.

"Nope."

"Liar."

Benji smirks but turns his attention back to the computer. I sigh, putting my glasses back on and looking over the numbers on the screen. None of it makes sense, even though it seems he has some sort of system with it. "What do these numbers mean?"

"I thought you were listening." My eyes flash to him, and he lifts a brow, his smirk growing.

"Shut the hell up and tell me what this means," I say, bumping his shoulder.

"Your sales have increased." I cock an eyebrow, disbelief swimming through me. Benji chuckles, leaning forward and pointing at the screen. The numbers swim together, and I blink trying to focus them. "Yeah, by about 20%."

"So, having Zach in the store is actually bringing people in?"

"I told you, Alex." Benji flips over the paperwork in front of him and begins comparing numbers between them and the computer. "Customers like to see the store open when they can actually make it in—after work."

"Does this mean we can hire more help?" I ask. My phone rings, and I fish it out as I listen to Benji.

"Not yet, but soon," he replies. "Do you have someone in mind?"

"No," I reply, glancing at the screen. Leslie's name flashes, and I hit ignore before tucking it back into my pocket. "But Zach's asking for a couple afternoons off."

Healing with You

"He's a teenager; of course he wants time off." Benji laughs, looking out the window. "You know, decorating would probably help bring in more customers too."

"I'll keep that in mind," I say, running a hand through my hair. That was the first thing Jana had pointed out when we met—the lack of decorations. I smile a little at the memory. "Are you still good to watch the girls tonight? Jana is coming here to help me pick out prizes for the booth."

Benji's eyes have locked onto something outside, and I'm not sure if he heard me. I wave a hand in front of his face, and he clears his throat, pushing away from the counter.

"Yeah, I'm looking forward to movie night with them," he says, crouching down to gather Harper's leash. He typically leaves her off leash unless he's in town. There are too many variables, he says. His eyes go back to the front window, a dark shadow crossing his face. "Did Wren tell you why she couldn't watch the girls? Is it her mom?"

"I'm not sure," I reply, glancing out toward the street. The reason for his concern becomes evident when I notice the small blonde standing a few feet away from the door, bundled tightly in a warm coat and a green scarf. Her hair flies out in a chaotic mess as she talks animatedly into her cell. "She just said she couldn't today. Why don't you go out and ask her?"

He's already moving before I say the words, Harper following closely behind him. "I'll come get the girls at five—is that okay?"

"Sure. Thanks, Benj," I say, but he's already out the door.

I watch him for a moment. He hops down the stairs, a move I'm sure hurt his knee, and smiles that carefree grin. Wren's tense shoulders relax, and she quickly gets off the phone as Benji approaches her. It's fascinating to see them, so obviously in love yet refusing to move past a simple friendship. How important she must be to him for him to willingly allow himself to stay in the friendzone just so he won't lose her.

He throws his arm around her shoulders, and they walk down the street together, a smile on both their faces. I watch until they disappear from my view, wondering if I could ever be *just* friends with someone I love.

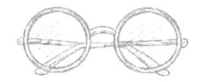

The sun sinks below the horizon as I close out the till, the small bell above the door ringing out in the deserted shop. I lift my head, ready to call out that we're closed, when I catch sight of the intruder. It's Jana, her dark curls flying freely around her face and her round cheeks flushed a pretty pink from the cold. She's backlit by the setting sun, her eyes bright and excited as she meets my gaze.

"Alex!" She's breathless, her chest heaving as she inhales a lungful of air. Simply seeing her sets my heart racing, and I too have to catch my breath. "Sorry I'm late! I just got back from the printers and look what I got!"

She holds out a brown box, and I take it, unable to hide the grin her excitement triggers. I open it, finding neatly stacked gift certificates inside. The Little Button Bakery logo takes up a third of each certificate, with the words '*Harmony Christmas Festival: Valid for ONE free dessert*' taking up the rest.

"Quinn said she'll sign them if Mrs. F isn't back in time," she adds, shrugging off her coat. I'm glad to see it's a new one, not the lightweight windbreaker she typically wears.

"These are adorable," I say. Her cheeks grow darker, and she tucks loose curls behind her ear. *You're adorable.* My chest tightens, and I drag my attention back to the gift certificates. "I stopped by Feldman's on my lunch break and grabbed some brown paper and twine. I hope that'll work."

"That's perfect, actually," Jana says, pulling at the hem of her oversized Columbia sweater. My eyes follow her as she walks toward the shelves closest to the windows. "You know, you should set up a display right here in front for any extras you have after the festival."

"That's a good idea." I set the coupon box on the coffee table in the center of the reading area, my palms already sweating. Jana glances around, her eyes lingering on the window. I can see she wants to ask about the decorations, or lack thereof, but she bites the corner of her lip. "I was thinking we could start with twenty books—do you think that'll be enough?"

"Yeah, that's probably a good place to start." She nods to herself, scanning the shelves nearest her as she nibbles at the corner of her thumb. "The festival is three days long, so we can gauge interest day one and go from there. And like I said, you could totally set up a cute display after the festival for any that don't sell."

"Alright, that sounds reasonable."

We fall quiet, and it begins to feel like an awkward teenage first date. I take the moment to study her. She stands with her shoulders back, her chin up, yet she nervously chews on her thumb, her hair hiding half her face as she studies the shelf beside her. She's an enigma, and I want nothing more than to dig deeper to find the truth of her.

After another minute of silence, I clear my throat, and she drags her eyes to my face, dropping her hand to her side abruptly.

"I guess we should decide which books to do," she says, tousling her hair. She steps around the couch, her cinnamon and honey scent invading my space as she gets closer. "I think we should stick to novels but have a decent variety."

"So, some mystery, some horror," I say, trying to focus on the project. It's difficult when she gets close enough to feel her warmth. It's brief, and as she steps past me, I try not to inhale too deeply. Her scent lingers, tempting me even as she walks toward the young adult fiction section.

"Some fantasy, some romance," she says with a nod, tossing a smile over her shoulder. "You get the idea. And then, once we have the books picked out, we can start brainstorming basic descriptions. That's probably going to be the toughest part of this whole project."

"That should be pretty simple," I say, watching as she begins pulling books off the shelves. She's got four in her arms by the time I make it to her side. "Here, let me carry those."

Her lips twitch in amusement, but she hands them over. I follow behind her as she moves to a new section and begins pulling more options.

"Do you read a lot?" she asks as she crouches down to get a thriller from the lower shelves.

"Just the books the girls ask for," I reply honestly. I've never been a big reader, only ever reading books required for college. Laura would read out loud to me before bed, in an attempt to get me interested in reading, but my dyslexia made it difficult to focus on the words. I loved hearing her voice, so I never complained, but I haven't touched a novel since.

"But you own a bookstore?" A short, shocked laugh. Jana's expression is a mixture of confusion and amusement as she turns to a new section—historical fiction.

"It was my wife's dream."

We both fall silent, and I realize how little I've told Jana about Laura. *Nothing*, actually. All she knows came from two sad little girls who miss their mother. Uncertainty fills me, overwhelming guilt coming back full force as I stand so close to Jana. My brain screams at me that I'm cheating on my wife.

"I'm going to take these to the front," I say, lifting the stack of books. Jana nods, her cheeks tinged a light pink and her eyes wide. I grit my teeth, hating how confusing this situation is and how uncomfortable I've made her. The urge to fix it swells as she fiddles with the armband of her sweater. "Are you hungry?"

"Oh, um..." She looks down at her hands then back to the shelves she was scanning through moments before.

"I haven't eaten in hours," I say, offering a small smile. "I can order some Chinese while you pick out the rest of the books—how does that sound?"

"Amazing, actually," she says, reciprocating the smile. I begin walking back to the front but pause before I get too far. Jana's already turned her attention to the bookshelf, her fingers walking over the spines of each book. She's so at peace amidst the books, like she was meant to live amongst them. She pulls out a book, and I shake my head, clearing the fog that tries to take over.

"Is there something specific you like?" I ask. Jana looks up from the book she's studying, a small smile playing on her lips again.

"Cashew chicken is my favorite," she says, tucking her hair as it falls again.

"Perfect." I hurry to the front of the shop and drop the books onto the coffee table beside her box of coupons. I fish my phone out of my pocket and make the call to order the food. After paying over the phone, I sink into the couch and rub a hand over my face.

Jana's still in the back, and I'm grateful. The war between my head and my heart rages on, each screaming at me. Before I know it, I'm hitting the call button on my phone and listening to it ring.

"Alex, I thought you were on a date," Benji says, and I shake my head, already questioning calling him.

"Not a date," I bite out, glancing at the shelves I know Jana stands behind.

"Okay, whatever you say, brother." He laughs. "Why are you calling? Is it over already?"

"I need advice," I say in a hushed tone. This is new territory to me, but I've watched Benji keep his feelings in check with Wren for the last five years. If anyone can give me advice, it's him.

"On dating?" he asks, humor filling his voice. "I know it's been a while, but—"

"Red light, Ben."

The phrase shuts him up, and I hear a long sigh through the phone. It was a brilliant idea from when we were teens, a codeword to tell the other when we needed him to be serious. If there was ever a situation where I needed Benji serious, it was this one. I spare another glance at the stacks where Jana is and run a hand down my face.

"Okay, what's up?"

"I don't know what the hell I'm supposed to do, Ben." Fear is choking me, keeping me from making a decision.

"About what, Alex?" he asks. I shake my head, trying to articulate my problem.

"This guilt—" I break off, breathing out deeply. Admitting to my growing feelings for Jana and the resulting guilt makes everything a little too real, and I'm not sure I'm ready for that.

"Alex," Benji sighs, and I drop my head back against the couch. "Laura's gone."

Tears prick at my eyes. "I know."

"She wouldn't want you to seclude yourself." There's a pause. "Or the girls."

"I can't..." I blow out a breath and clench my jaw, trying to hold back the tears. "I love her, Benji. I love Laura, and it hurts so much."

"I know, brother."

"But Jana..." The tightness in my chest releases a little, and I shake my head again. I lower my voice further. "There's something about her; I can't get her out of my head, Ben. She makes everything feel...right. Like she's the piece I've been missing."

"You're allowed to fall in love again, Alex."

"But I can't shake this feeling—it feels like I'm betraying Laura by even looking at Jana."

"You know that's not what's happening," Benji says lowly. *Do I?* "There is no doubt in anyone's mind that you love Laura. But Alex, she's not here anymore. She's gone and you're still here. You deserve to be happy, and if Jana is how you get there, then Laura would want you to take a chance."

"I don't know how, Ben."

"You start by letting her in."

CHAPTER THIRTEEN
ALEX

Benji's words linger in my mind. Could he be right? Would Laura want me to move on? I sigh and toss my phone onto the coffee table before leaning back on the couch. I'm physically drained and mentally overwhelmed from the conversation. I rest my head against the back of the couch and close my eyes, drawing Laura's face to the forefront of my mind.

She'd always been beautiful, with large, almond-shaped hazel eyes framed by long lashes. She was blemish free, no freckles or dark spots on her clear skin, and her smile was wide and happy. Always happy. I remember her blonde hair, soft and tangle-free, sitting just above her slender shoulders.

She was the exact opposite of Jana.

Jana.

I open my eyes, finding her face easily. She's just walking out of the shelves, her eyes trained on the pile of books in her arms. She looks pleased with herself, her full lips tilted up in a soft smile, and as she lifts her head, I'm rendered breathless.

Her dark curls are unruly, her cheeks tinged pink, her big brown eyes alight with excitement. She walks to my side, setting the precariously balanced books on the edge of the coffee table before sagging onto the couch. She rests her head against the back of the couch and sighs out a deep breath.

"I picked a few more than the agreed upon twenty books, but…" She grins, rolling her head toward me.

"We can create a display with the extras," I finish, nodding with a laugh. "So, what's the next step now that we've picked out the books?"

She pushes herself up and begins sorting the books into different piles.

"Next, we've got to come up with a basic description for each book." She holds up a thicker book, a creepy looking staircase on the cover. "For example, this one is a supernatural thriller about a guy who can see ghosts and demons who are possessing people, and his journey to self-healing while battling a being who wants him dead."

"You read thrillers?" I ask, my surprise obvious. She laughs.

"On occasion."

"Honestly, I had you pegged as a romance girl."

She raises an eyebrow, her lips quirking up in an amused smirk. "Oh, I'm definitely a romance girly—take this one." She holds up another book. "This is a mafia romance with grief and guilt—just absolutely heartbreaking, really. But anyway, the two leads are so broken, like ridiculously so, and they end up helping each other heal while they deal with their issues. Oh, and it's spicy."

"Spicy?" I laugh, enjoying seeing her in her element. Our eyes lock, and there's something in my gut that screams at me to get closer. Her cheeks flush deeply, and she looks away quickly.

"Oh, that just means there's explicit sex scenes in the novel." She fiddles with the armband of her sweater. "We need to make sure we note that on the books with any sort of spice."

"And you know which of these need that note?" I ask, adding a soft teasing to my tone. Her blush deepens as she nods, and a knowing smirk pulls at my lips. "That's a good girl."

Her breath catches audibly in her throat, her eyes wide and her lips parting in an adorable little gasp. I've never wanted to kiss someone as badly as I do in this moment, sitting so close, our knees bump together and cinnamon fills my senses.

There's a sharp knock on the glass door, breaking the intense eye contact we share and drawing both of our attention to the front of the shop. The delivery boy stands huddled on the stairs, and it takes me a moment to bring myself to stand up. If I hadn't promised to feed her, I would leave him to freeze outside and give my full attention to the gorgeous woman beside me.

Instead, I move to the door. I fish my wallet out of my pocket and pull out a few bills, handing them to the kid as I open the door. He hands over the food, a smile lighting up his face when he sees the tip.

"Thanks, Mister."

"Sure thing, kid," I reply, glancing at the fresh snowfall outside. "Stay warm out there."

I close the door, making sure it's still locked before turning back to Jana. She's fiddling with the stacks of books in front of her, moving them around to clear space for the food. I sit beside her, setting the brown paper bag on the table and begin pulling out the boxes.

"That smells delicious," she says, breaking the silence between us. I smile, ignoring the irritation from the delivery boy's interruption. It's probably a good thing I didn't kiss her, especially considering I can't shake this guilt.

"I hope you're hungry,"

"I'm starved," she says, her cheeks flushing as she bites her bottom lip. "I was so distracted with the bakery and then the gift certificates…I forgot to eat lunch."

I turn to look at her, raising my brows in surprise. "You haven't eaten since this morning?"

She shakes her head sheepishly, a nervous laugh slipping past her lips. She sits forward, her hands trapped between her thick thighs as one leg bounces. It's obvious she's nervous—uncomfortable, even—so I smile gently and offer her a set of chopsticks.

"Well then," I say, pushing the cashew chicken across the table. "Allow me to be of service—I can't let my guest go hungry."

She smiles, tucking her hair behind her ear as it falls in front of her eyes again. "Thank you, Alex."

I love hearing my name roll from her tongue. It sends my heart racing, and my blood feels like it's boiling in my veins. Heat floods through my body as I watch her split her chopsticks before sinking to the floor in front of the couch. I swallow roughly, tearing my eyes away from the glint of hunger in her eyes. Everything she does makes me want her more, and it's slowly driving me insane.

I turn my attention to my own food, trying to ignore the little moans of satisfaction that come from the woman before me. I grit my teeth, suddenly not hungry for Chinese food.

"How did you hear about our little town?" I ask finally, breaking the silence. My voice is strained, but I don't think Jana notices it. She swallows a mouthful of chicken, a smile brightening her face.

"Actually, I grew up here," she says, fiddling with her chopsticks. Surprise takes over, temporarily relieving the painful attraction. Jana chuckles. "I grew up in the Bloom Gardens neighborhood—just a few streets down from you, actually."

"What a small world," I say, poking at my own chicken. "Does your dad still live there?"

"No." Her smile falters, her eyes misting over. She looks down at her lap and takes a deep breath. "No, he died in the same car accident that killed my mom six years ago. I was..." She pauses, shaking her head. "I was away at college when it happened."

"Jana, I—"

"It's okay," she says, shaking her head. Her warm brown eyes are full of tears, but still, she smiles. "You had no way of knowing."

"I'm so sorry." And I am. Losing a parent couldn't be easy but losing them both at the same time—that had to have been horrible.

"I haven't been back since their funeral," Jana says softly, her voice breaking a little. She laughs sadly, wiping the corner of her eyes before going back to pushing around her food. My heart aches for her loss, empathy rolling through me. "I didn't really have a reason to, I guess. My sister, Katy... She moved away long before our parents died; married some guy in finance and had a kid. I haven't seen her in years."

"What brought you back now?" I ask, setting my box of chicken on the table. She bites out a laugh, shaking her head again. She works her jaw, a glint of anger flashing in her eyes.

"I couldn't stay in Louisiana," she says, setting her food down. She rests an elbow on the couch cushion, leaning her head in her palm and tucking her legs under herself. She sighs out a sharp breath. "Hadlee's pretty much all I've got left in this world, so when she asked me to come stay after I lost my job...it was a no-brainer."

"I'm sorry, Jana. That must be difficult." I lean forward to study Jana's face, resting my elbows on my knees. Her micro-expressions give away more than I think she realizes. "I can't imagine life without my family—especially Benji."

"Is it just the two of you?" she asks, dragging a hand through her curls. They flop to the side, leaving her neck exposed. Her creamy skin is soft, I know from past experiences, and I have to drag my eyes back to hers before I get too distracted by the enticing view.

I shake my head. "Nah, we have a younger sister—Carlee. She lives in Washington, near our parents."

"Alex, Benji, and Carlee?" She laughs, her eyes crinkling in the corners. I'm glad she's found humor in the conversation, her tears mostly dry. "Was the alphabet thing on purpose, or just how things turned out?"

"Oh, definitely on purpose," I say, smiling with her. My eyes drop to my hands, clasped in front of me, my wedding band glaring harshly back at me as I twist it absently. There's a sharp pain in my chest at the reminder, and I shake my head. "So was the 'M' thing with my girls."

"Did your wife's name start with an 'M'?" Jana asks softly. The realization that I've not even told her Laura's name hits me square in the chest, and I feel like the breath has been knocked out of my lungs. That familiar guilt creeps in, and Benji's words come back to me. *Start by letting her in.* I shift uncomfortably, inhaling a sharp breath.

"No, um…" I trail off, shaking my head as the familiar ache settles in my chest. I try to smile, but I fail and clear my throat instead. "Her name was Laura."

"Will you tell me about her?"

The question knocks me off guard. Thoughts and memories I've kept locked away for two years come rushing back, flooding my mind with images of Laura's life intertwined with mine. There's no way to express the years of love and heartache, joy and sadness that we shared—nor the pain that fills me anytime I think of her.

"What do you want to know?"

"Anything—everything," Jana says, placing a hand over mine. Her touch is warm and comforting, and as the soft pads of her fingers smooth over my clenched fists, I feel myself beginning to relax. I lift my gaze, meeting warm brown eyes that hold an understanding I can't quite make sense of. "Sometimes, talking about those we've loved and lost can help ease the ache we feel in our hearts. So…tell me about Laura—how did you meet?"

"College," I say, sending my mind back all those years ago. "She was in my sophomore English Lit class. She was brilliant, knew the answer to everything." I smile. "It drove me nuts, since none of it made a lick of sense to me. Actually, she ended up tutoring me—I *definitely* got the better end of that deal."

"I bet," Jana says with a laugh. "When did you finally ask her out?"

"Our second tutoring session." I smile at the memory. Laura's blonde hair had fallen into her eyes as she read from the book, and I'd reached across the table to push it back. Her hazel eyes were startled when she met my gaze, a shy smile taking over her expression once the words were out of my mouth. "Once I got to know her...everything just felt right. We got married my senior year at Brown."

"How long were you married?"

"Eight years." The ache in my chest seems to grow, thinking about how our time together was cut short in such a terrible way. I swallow past the lump in my throat. "Maddie came about a year after we were married, then Morgan nineteen months later."

"They're beautiful," Jana says, a sincere smile on her face. "And brilliant, too."

There's no doubt in my mind that Jana cares for my daughters. I've seen the way she looks at them, like she could easily love them forever. My heart pounds in my chest, knowing that's exactly what they need—not just someone to love and adore them, but a mother figure to help them as they grow into young women.

"They take after Laura," I say, trying to break the growing tension between us. I shake my head with a self-deprecating laugh.

"They take after you, too, Alex," Jana says softly. I clench my jaw, hating how quickly the emotions take over. There's more to the story, more to share, but the words stick in my throat. Pressure builds behind my eyes, and I grip Jana's hand, lacing our fingers together. It surprises both of us, I think, but thankfully, she doesn't pull away. She simply squeezes my hand, encouraging me to continue.

"Laura—" I cut myself off, the anger and pain swelling up in my chest like they did the day she died. It takes me a moment to compose myself enough to continue, Jana waiting patiently. "Laura died giving birth to our son."

"*Oh my God.*" On her breathless whisper, the dam breaks. Tears blur my vision, a sob climbing up my throat. "Oh, Alex…"

Her touch is gentle on my face, her fingertips dragging through the tears on my cheeks. I haven't cried like this since the doctor told me there was nothing more they could do; my wife hadn't made it through the birth.

"Maddox lived for an hour." My voice breaks, and it's all I can do to stay upright. Jana's warmth seeps into me as she crawls between my legs and wraps her arms around my waist. Her honey and cinnamon scent floods my senses, and I suck in a deep breath. It's comforting, and I pull her closer, wrapping my arms around her. She presses her head against my chest, and I tuck my face in her hair, each of us taking comfort in the other.

Jana pulls away first, and when our eyes meet, something inside me clicks into place. I search her face, trying to understand what changed, but all I see is her uncertainty. I keep my hands on her arms, enjoying the warmth of her against me. *This is okay.*

"Alex, I..." she trails off, shaking her head. "I can't even imagine the pain you're holding. I'm so, so sorry, and I know that doesn't help, but I have no other words to express my sympathy."

"You don't need other words, Jana," I say, standing and pulling her up with me. Her chest brushes mine, and I want nothing more than to pull her into me and hold her forever. "I don't think you understand how much you've done for me tonight. Thank you. Thank you for sitting in my grief with me, for letting me share."

"*Of course*, Alex," she breathes out, empathy seeping into her voice. "As humans, we need to share our emotions with others. It's not healthy to bottle it up, so I'm really glad you felt comfortable sharing with me."

"It's easy with you," I say softly. I lift my hand to her cheek, pushing the curls behind her ear like she's been doing all night. Her breath catches in her throat, our eyes locking on each other. *Everything has been so easy with her*. I lean forward, resting my forehead against hers, still caressing her cheek softly. Our breathing mingles, and I can feel my heart pound anxiously against my ribs.

Thinking over the last few weeks, everything seemed to push me to Jana: our first meeting here, being assigned to the same booth—perhaps this *is* fate. Perhaps *Jana* is the answer to my prayers for a happy Christmas.

"It's getting late," Jana says, breaking the silence we've fallen into. She takes a step back, putting space between us. "I suppose we can finish this project another day."

I don't look away from her, even though she turns away, gathering her things. She moves quickly, her movements jerky, and when she turns back to me, she's gnawing on her bottom lip.

"Do you need a ride?" I ask.

"No, that's okay." She smiles shyly, her cheeks flaring pink. "Hadlee lent me her car for the night."

I nod, disappointed. The drive to her house is only about eight minutes from here, but that's eight minutes I could spend with her. She walks to the front door, and I follow. She pauses to pull her coat on. "I'll call you later then, to schedule a time to finish with the books?"

"Yeah, that's fine," she says, looking up at me with a smile. "I'll see you later, Alex."

I lean down, pressing a soft yet firm kiss to her forehead, reveling in the softness of her skin and the hitch in her breath. I linger there for a moment, inhaling the scent of honey and cinnamon, before pulling away and meeting her gaze once more. Her big brown eyes are wide, her full pink lips parted in surprise, and it takes everything in me not to capture them in a kiss right now. Instead, I smile gently.

"See you later, darling."

CHAPTER FOURTEEN
JANA

It's a cold Saturday morning, and I wake up wanting to bake. I pull my Columbia sweater over my head and tug on some warm wool socks before padding out to the kitchen. I can hear Hadlee's even breathing as I pass her bedroom, the door cracked a tiny bit. I peek in, finding my friend still asleep, sprawled out on her king-sized bed. I smile and pull the door closed the rest of the way before heading out into the main living space.

The lights from the Christmas tree illuminate the top of the piano and the immediate surrounding area, and as the grey light of day makes its way through the front windows, I feel a surge of joy fill me. Christmas was always my favorite holiday, but since the loss of my parents, I've avoided everything to do with the holiday. Being back here, in Harmony, I can't help but feel that joy returning.

But it's not just Harmony affecting me.

I grab an apron from the kitchen drawer and set the oven to preheat.

Alex's expression the other night, full of wonder and acceptance, was burned into my head. I was completely destroyed when he shared how Laura died and knowing he's been holding onto that makes everything click into place for me. He's been protecting his heart from getting broken again, and knowing he trusted me enough to share those emotions…

I pull a large bowl out of the cupboard, then reach for a wooden spoon before searching the pantry. Hadlee's made sure to keep it well stocked, knowing I tend to bake at all times of the day—which means she reaps the rewards. Sugar and flour go to the counter, and I dig around for the last dry ingredients until I find them.

Measuring out the dry ingredients, I try to keep my thoughts off the man who's occupied them since I returned to Harmony. It's pointless, though. The feeling of his calloused hand caressing my cheek, his forehead pressing against mine…

I sigh out a big breath, my hand shaking as I pour the flour into the bowl. It was the second time I thought he would kiss me, but it was me who pulled away first this time. There's no doubt in my mind that Alex would love hard and deep if he wanted to, but me…I'm not ready for a love like that. And if I'm honest, I don't think I've ever been ready for the kind of true love Alex obviously has for Laura.

Jon and George were only part of my tragic history, and I still haven't moved past those betrayals. How could I let myself love someone so wonderful when I'm the last person who could love him right? While my love for his daughters has grown exponentially, even in the short time we've known each other, I don't know if I could love him the way he deserves.

I add butter to the bowl, my heart feeling a little more bruised than it was when I first woke up. Shortening, salt, and a splash of water are added to the bowl, and I begin mixing it together, forming a dough. I shake my head, clearing the unwanted thoughts as I manhandle the mixture.

"Oooh, what are you making?" Hadlee asks. I look up, surprised to see her leaning against the counter in front of me. Her dark hair is tied on top of her head in a messy bun, her t-shirt hanging off her shoulder.

"Apple pie." Alex's voice fills my head, his words from last week stuck in my head. *'I love apple pie.'* I form the dough into a ball and wrap it in plastic wrap before tucking it into the fridge. Wiping my hands on my apron, I reach for the pile of apples and begin peeling them with a knife.

"Are you alright, Jay?" she asks, concern filling her husky sleep voice. I shrug, forcing a smile to my lips.

"Just been thinking," I reply. It's true—my thoughts have already made my day take a sour turn, and it's not even ten a.m.

"That's never a good idea," Hadlee says, shaking her head. "Especially not on a Saturday."

A laugh slips out, and I nod in agreement. "I really shouldn't bake alone, or I'll ruin both our days with my thinking."

"Do you want to talk about it?" she asks, perching on a barstool and reaching for an apple. She wiggles her fingers at me, and I roll my eyes, passing the peeler to her. As she begins peeling the rest of the apples, I grab a cutting board and knife to begin slicing them. "You know you always feel better after you talk it out."

"I don't know, Lee," I say, wiping my arm over my forehead. "It's stupid, really."

"Well." She waves the peeler in my face, a teasing smile on her lips. "We can talk now, or I can call Wren and Q, and you can talk when they get here."

I glare harshly at the apple I just started on, feeling irritation bubbling beneath my skin. Hadlee means well, I know that, but I'm not sure I'm confident in talking about this situation with her—or our other friends right now. How am I supposed to tell her I'm in over my head here? That I want to disappear again and never come back?

"Jana, you know I'm here for you, right?"

"Of course," I say, looking up from where I'm slivering apples, my knife pausing halfway through the fruit. "I'm just…ugh…it's complicated?"

"Complicated?" Hadlee tilts her head, a small, sad smile on her face. "Or just scary?"

I blow out a breath, tears prickling in my eyes as I try to focus on the task at hand. I blink through the tears, and they fall, hitting the wooden cutting board and soaking into it. "I told you, it's stupid."

"Your feelings aren't stupid, Jana," she says softly, setting her tools down.

"My heart hurts, Lee," I say, hating how vulnerable and *weak* I sound. "I'm terrified to let myself fall in love, to even entertain the idea of loving someone, when all I've ever had is heartbreak."

"Alex isn't like that, Jay."

"Alex deserves more than this," I say, gesturing to myself. I chuckle wryly, wiping the tears with my sleeve. "Alex and Maddie and Morgan...they've been through so much, and they deserve someone who can love them without this...this..."

"Fear?"

"Exactly," I breathe out. Biting my lip, I shake my head. "I'm afraid of love, Hadlee. I'm afraid to let myself be vulnerable and trust someone that way again."

"That's completely understandable, Jana," she replies. "You've had horrible experiences—but that's not what love is. Jon didn't love you, Jay, and neither did George. Love is...love is pure. It's dropping everything to be there for the other person when they need you. It's sharing your deepest, darkest fears and dreams. It's trusting each other, accepting each other, no matter what."

There's a pause, and I hold back the sob that begs to be released.

"It's baking them a pie because they mentioned in passing that they love it." Her whisper breaks me, and the sob is released. I crumble to the floor, the knife clattering to the counter and my heart aches in my chest as waves of emotions flood over me. Anger at Jon and George for never truly loving me, disgust in myself for holding onto them so tightly when I knew things were going wrong. Fear of falling for someone whose love for his late wife keeps him from moving on. Regret for not being able to love his daughters without falling for him as well.

"I can't—" I choke on the tears, shaking my head. Hadlee is beside me, one hand smoothing back my hair while the other wraps around my shoulders.

"Love isn't something you can control, Jana," she says softly, leaning her cheek on the top of my head. "And life without love is just pointless."

"But how, Hadlee?" I ask, desperate for an answer to the question that's been plaguing me for weeks. "How do I open myself to the possibility of finding love—especially with where I'm coming from? I don't know if I can trust someone with my heart again. It's so fucking broken—I'm broken."

"You're not broken, Jay."

Despite her assurances, I know the truth. I've been broken for far longer than either of us realizes.

The meticulous basket weave takes my focus, and I allow the ease of working the dough into a pattern to soothe my frayed nerves. This is the final step before I pop the pie into the oven, and I want it to be perfect. I delicately swipe a layer of egg whites over the top crust before sliding the pie into the oven and setting the timer.

Hadlee sits on the floor in the living room, leaning against the piano as she fiddles with a bow on the gift she just finished wrapping. There's a mess of paper and ribbons surrounding her, a testament to her entire lifestyle, really.

"Are you planning to see Katy for Christmas?" she asks, lifting her eyes to mine. I'm surprised by her question, knocked off kilter once more by the unexpected emotions it brings up. I drop my gaze to the messy counter, my hands instinctively moving to clean as I pull my bottom lip between my teeth. A sharp pain blooms when I bite down, the taste of blood strong on my tongue.

My sister and I haven't spoken in years; not since our parents' funeral six years ago. Even before then, our relationship had been strenuous, but the icing on the cake was when she married a narcissistic asshole who hated my guts—all because I caught him in a compromising position with Katy's best friend a few weeks before the wedding. I tried to tell Katy of his infidelity, but she chose to believe him over me and had effectively written me off. They'd even uninvited me to the wedding.

I knew she had a baby some years ago, but I still don't know if it was a boy or girl, or what they named it. My heart cracks when I think of all the missed holidays and birthdays over the years. That child would be about Morgan's age by now, a thought that sends a rush of sadness through me.

"No, I don't think so." I don't have the collateral to pretend, not now, and not with Hadlee. No matter how much I might want to see and interact with my sister, she never picks up the phone. She may have even changed her number at this point. "I'm not sure I can handle another rejection this year."

"She still won't answer your calls?"

"Katy's a stubborn girl," I say with a small sigh, rinsing out the bowls I used and tucking them into the dishwasher. Stubborn is one word for it. Hot-headed is another. "Even if that asshole would let her answer, I don't think her ego would."

"I'm sorry, Jay."

I shrug, washing my hands before walking into the living room and dropping onto the couch. I sink into the cushions, allowing the comfort to ease my achy body.

"What about you?" I ask, leaning my head against the armrest. "Any plans with the family?"

Hadlee's snort is so unladylike, I almost laugh. She briefly peers at me through her lashes before letting her eyes drop back to the new gift she's wrapping. "As if."

"That bad?"

"Worse." She shakes her head, tugging a little too hard at the paper. It tears in half, and she groans, cursing low under her breath. "Dad and Step-Momster decided to go on a cruise in the Caribbean with their love child and his family, while Mom and her new boyfriend, *Samson*, have invited me to eat tofurky and go surfing in Cali. *Samson*, what the hell kind of name is that? And who actually likes tofurky?"

"A sisters' Christmas it is," I say with a laugh.

"I'm hoping that means you're baking gingerbread cookies and we're ordering Chinese," Hadlee says, pointing the scissors at me. She wears the most serious expression on her face, and I grin.

"And we'll watch *It's a Wonderful Life*."

"Thank God. I can't wait for the festival to be over," Hadlee says, ripping off a piece of tape. "I'm pretty sure the Casey's Cuts/Feldman's booth is going to be the worst one this town has seen in a long time."

"Oh yeah? What are you guys doing?"

"Oh, nothing as amazingly adorable as your prize wheel and books," she says, giving me a knowing smile. "I think Joey Feldman has lost his ever-loving mind. He wants to do a carnival strength game. He's building the thing instead of ordering one, and I have no idea what we're supposed to do for prizes for that."

"Gift cards?"

"I tried to suggest incorporating the businesses into it, but he's shut all of my ideas down." She shrugs, wrapping a spare ribbon around the gift she just wrapped. "I swear, if I ever get paired with a Feldman again, I'm going to gouge my eyes out."

"At least it's not Donnelly," I tease. Hadlee rolls her eyes with a half-hearted laugh.

"*Donnelly* moved to Missoula four years ago," she says. "Which is fine. I couldn't take the adoration and admittedly slightly creepy semi-stalking anymore."

"*Slightly* creepy?" I laugh. "Lee, he showed up at your house after you got your wisdom teeth removed and convinced your dad he was your boyfriend. In fact, I think I still have the photos he took of you, jaw all swollen and drugged to hell."

"Okay, so he was obsessed," she pauses, adjusting the bow on each wrapped gift one more time. "But who doesn't love a little obsession every once in a while? I actually kinda miss the kid offering to carry my schoolbooks and following us around like a lost puppy."

"High school was a long time ago, Hadlee."

"I know, it's just..." She shakes her head, a wistful smile playing on her lips as her fingers trail over the ribbons. "I miss how simple it was, you know?"

I nod, sinking further into the couch. High school was the simplest time of my life, despite how difficult it seemed at the time. Katy and I were still friends, Mom and Dad were still alive, and all my problems were simply trivial. Oh, yes...I miss how simple high school was, too.

Hadlee stands and sets the gifts beneath the tree at the same moment my timer goes off. I push to my feet and hurry to pull the pie out of the oven and set it on the counter. The crust is a delightful golden-brown color, and my mouth instantly waters at the burst of cinnamon and apple.

"So, what are you going to do with the pie?" Hadlee asks, leaning against the counter once more. I meet her gaze and bite my lip. What *am* I going to do with the pie?

"I-I don't know," I say, uncertainty flooding through me. Alex's words from last week prompted me to make it, but now that I've admitted my fear aloud, I'm not sure what to do. That family deserves more than what I have to offer, more than my broken heart and wounded soul. Those girls deserve the world, and Alex...Alex deserves someone who can love him with everything in their soul. *But that's not me.*

As if she can read my thoughts, Hadlee reaches across the counter and grabs my hand, squeezing it with all her might. "There's no harm in trying, Jay," she says. "Take the pie and go—be *vulnerable*. Tell him how you feel, with no expectations or stipulations and see what happens."

"I don't know if I can, Lee." My chest feels tight as I think about going to Alex's home and ambushing him like that. The tentative friendship between us has become incredibly important to me; losing *that* would hurt more than him not feeling the same way I do. Anxiety threatens to overwhelm me, my fingers tapping a halting pattern against the countertop. *Tap, tap, tap. Tap. Tap, tap, tap.*

"You've got to try, Jana," Hadlee says, pushing her keys into my hand. "Just go and see what happens. It's okay to be scared, but you can't let the fear keep you from finding real, true happiness."

I stand on Alex's front porch, the oak wood door staring back at me as I try to talk myself into knocking. It took twice as long as it normally would have to get here, the entire drive filled with an internal argument, and *apparently*, I'm still not completely convinced this is the right decision. The pie is balanced precariously in one hand, the other poised to knock, when suddenly, the door swings open, and I'm now staring directly into those gorgeous amber eyes.

"Jana!" The surprise is obvious, his eyes wide, but the smile that blooms there fills me with warmth until I'm all-but a gooey puddle before him. "What are you doing here?"

"Oh, um..." I blink through the daze and smile awkwardly, lifting the dish in my hands. "I made you a pie."

His eyes drop to my hands, and the smile grows. "I love apple pie."

"I know."

We stare at each other, unspoken words lingering in the air around us. There's a charge in the air, and I feel goosebumps prickle to life under his intense gaze. His lips part, tongue swiping over them, and he looks like he's going to say something important. I hold my breath, the fear of rejection lingering in the back of my mind.

"Miss Jana!" Maddie cries out. She jostles her father, pushing her way onto the porch as she smiles brightly up at me. She grabs my free hand, her little one fitting nicely into mine. "You're here! Daddy said he didn't think you could come!"

"Come?" I look from her excited face back up to Alex, and he shrugs apologetically.

"We're going ice skating." Morgan chimes in softly from her position beside her father. She clings shyly to his pant leg, her blonde hair tucked beneath a bubblegum pink beanie and her brown eyes peeking up at me. She giggles before ducking behind Alex's leg once more.

"Ice skating, huh?" I ask, smiling.

"Daddy said you had plans, 'cause it's Saturday," Maddie says, a small pout pulling at her lips. "But you're here now! So, can you? Can you come with us? Ooo, is that pie?"

Warmth spreads through my chest, and that lingering fear disappears as Maddie takes the pie from my hands. Tears prick at my eyes, and I don't try to fight my grin. She wants me around, wants to spend time with me despite my flaws and brokenness. This little girl doesn't see those things, and as I look between the little family, I realize that maybe none of them care about those things. Maybe they could love me—and I know I could easily love them.

"I'd love to go ice skating with you."

CHAPTER FIFTEEN
ALEX

Sharing with Jana closed a chapter I hadn't realized I'd been keeping open, and since that night, everything with her has felt attainable. I still love Laura, and I always will. She'll always hold a special place in my heart, but now...loving someone else doesn't seem so impossible. In fact, loving Jana is the only thing that feels real anymore.

My eyes are trained on her from across the ice rink, following her every move. She holds Maddie's hand as they circle the rink, big, bright smiles on their faces. Jana's bright red coat is easy to spot amidst the black and gray figures between us. Her dark curls hang loose around her face, and even from here I can see her glowing cheeks as she laughs with my daughter.

Warmth spreads through me, and I smile. I know she loves my daughters; I can see it in the way her eyes light up when she sees them, in the curve of her smile when they speak. *But could she love me?*

Morgan tugs on my hand, and I bring my attention back to her. She clings to me and the wall, her little gloved hands shaking as we move slowly around the rink. Her bright pink cap hides her hair and half her face, and as I crouch down to adjust it, she grins at me.

"Can we get hot chocolate, Daddy?" she asks sweetly.

"Sure thing, Bug." I take a moment to adjust her coat, pulling the zipper up to her chin. Morgan claps in excitement, her giggle bringing attention from those around us. I glance up, locking eyes on Jana and Maddie easily. Maddie has her eyes on us already, and waves enthusiastically as I stand. "Should we invite Maddie and Miss Jana to come with us?"

Morgan grips my hand tightly, waving to her sister with the same enthusiasm. We begin the lazy skate across the ice rink, doing our best to avoid the chaotic skaters. It's crowded, and a part of me regrets coming out on a Saturday, but the grins on my daughters' faces make the whole thing worth it.

"Daddy?" Morgan tugs me to a stop, her voice small in the din of the ice rink. "Do you think Miss Jana loves us?"

My eyes move from her face to the glowing smile Jana directs at Maddie. "Yeah, baby, I think she does."

"Are you gonna marry Miss Jana?"

The question catches me off guard, and I crouch in front of her, not caring if we're in the way. My heart hammers against its cage, my blood burning through my veins. *Marry Jana?* The image of Jana in a wedding dress, walking down the aisle, is almost too much for me, and I have to shove it into the recesses of my mind. My breathing is harsh, and I have to remember to control my tone. "Why are you asking that, Bug?"

"Maddie says that when you love someone, you marry them." She tilts her head in curiosity. "And she said Miss Jana is gonna be our new mama because you love her."

There's so much hope in Morgan's amber eyes that I fall onto my ass on the ice. She giggles, her nose crinkling in the same way Laura's used to. The memory of Maddie and Laura talking about what it meant to be married comes back to me. For weeks after, Maddie would bring me flowers and ask me to marry her, because she loved me.

"It's more complicated than that, Bug," I say, my voice hoarse. Swallowing past the lump forming in my throat, I hold her hands and pull her closer to me. "I can't marry Jana just because we love her. It takes more than just love for two people to get married."

Disappointment floods my five-year-old's face, and I can see the tears welling on her lashes. Her bottom lip quivers, and I know we're mere seconds from a full-blown meltdown.

"But I want you to marry Miss Jana," she cries, sadness filling her voice. I pull her into my arms, tucking her tightly against my chest as she begins to cry. Her little body shakes, and she hides her face in my neck. "I want her to be my mama so she can comb my hair and tuck me in at bedtime."

My heart cracks when I realize how attached to Jana my daughters have become. This isn't just about me and my happiness—it's about theirs as well. "That would be nice, wouldn't it, Bug?"

Morgan nods against my shoulder. I mutter softly to her, soothing words of comfort, but my mind is stuck on the idea of bringing Jana into our lives so permanently. It's a dangerous game because it's not just my heart on the line. There are three of us, and if things don't work out between Jana and me, it would be my daughters' fragile hearts that would be left in pieces.

"Should we get some hot chocolate now?"

Morgan cuddles into Jana's side, her eyes drooping tiredly, but a smile on her face, nonetheless. Jana uses one hand to smooth Morgan's blonde curls away from her face as she blows on Maddie's hot chocolate. I sit across from the three of them, holding my own cup of cocoa in front of my face.

"Here you go, love," Jana says, sliding the mug to Maddie.

"Thank you, Miss Jana," she says sweetly before breaking her sugar cookie into quarters. She takes a bite, chewing slowly. A little scowl forms between her brows, her nose wrinkling. "Miss Jana's cookies are better."

I meet Jana's eyes over the rim of my mug, a smile playing on my lips as her cheeks flush a pretty pink at the compliment from my seven-year-old. The steam of the hot drink warms my cheeks, and the smell of chocolate and peppermint fills my senses. *I wish I could smell her cinnamon and honey right now.* Jana's smile makes my stomach flip, and I feel like a schoolboy with a crush.

"Thank you, Maddie," she says with a smile.

"Do you make lots of cookies, Miss Jana?" Morgan asks. A big yawn takes over as Jana's fingers dance gently over the little girl's temple. She holds her cookie in one hand as her eyes droop closed, then fly open, only to drop closed once more.

"Sure do!" Jana says, stirring her own cocoa. "It's part of working at the bakery, but I love baking at home, too. I make sugar cookies, chocolate chip cookies—"

"Gingerbread?" Maddie asks, her hazel eyes hopeful. I have to smile, knowing how much my girls love sweets.

"Gingerbread is my favorite," Jana says conspiratorially, winking at Maddie.

"Mine too!" she giggles. I chuckle, shaking my head. Maddie loves *all* cookies.

"What about you Alex?" Jana asks. She looks at me through her lashes, a light blush evident on her cheeks as she smiles shyly at me. My gut tightens, warmth flooding me as her tongue darts out to wet her lips. My mouth is dry. "Do you have a favorite cookie?"

"Snickerdoodles." *Simply because cinnamon reminds me of you.*

"That's not true," Maddie says, and I swing my gaze away from Jana. Maddie's brow is furrowed, her little scowl firmly back in place. "His favorites are oatmeal with chocolate chip."

"Oh, are they?" Jana asks, a surprised laugh slipping out as she looks between us. I'm surprised too. The fact that Maddie might know my favorite cookie had never crossed my mind before.

"You're right, Mads," I say, tipping my head in surrender. "But I do enjoy a good snickerdoodle."

"Miss Jana..."

I watch them interact, barely hearing the switch in conversation. Maddie is talking about trains again, and I'm impressed by the focus Jana gives her. Never once do her eyes glaze over as she listens with rapt attention to the girl explaining the features of the new train she saw on TV. Morgan has fallen fast asleep, her head resting against Jana, her cookie forgotten on the table beside her cocoa.

My heart feels at peace here with them—with *Jana*. For the first time in a long time, I'm not focused on the grief of losing my wife and son. I twist my wedding band, watching Jana's lips tilt into a smile as Maddie makes a face, and Laura's voice rings in my head. *Love is why we're here, Alex. Don't let your stubbornness stop you from experiencing the very reason for our existence.*

I never received my copy of "*The Widower's Guide to Grief*", couldn't even find where to order it online. There were so many moments in the last two years when I would've given anything for someone to walk me through it. But it's not real. There *is* no manual to help you grieve. No guidelines, no deadlines...no timeline. There's no one around to tell you how long to grieve, or when it's okay to start loving someone else.

Sitting here now, watching Jana's lips tilt up as she throws her head back and lets out a belly laugh, I know. Everything about this woman screams to be loved, and in this moment, I think I'm done waiting. No matter what happens, I want her. And I'm ready to give her every bit of love that she deserves.

CHAPTER SIXTEEN
JANA

The spicy smell of gingerbread permeates the entire house, bringing the Christmas spirit to life within these four walls. I wipe the counter down, cleaning up the remaining evidence of my baking as I hum along to the music echoing through the house.

Spending yesterday afternoon with Alex and the girls brought a peace to my heart I hadn't realized I was missing. I spin around the kitchen, a smile permanently etched onto my face. Warmth fills me, and it feels like I'm being wrapped in a warm blanket. Whatever this feeling is, I would pay good money to keep it forever. For the first time in a very long time, I finally feel like myself.

"You're happy," Hadlee notes as she enters the open space. She fastens her earrings in place, watching me with a grin. My cheeks warm in a blush, but I can't deny her words. I *am* happy. "I'm so happy to see you smiling again."

"What are you talking about, *'smiling again'*?" I ask with a laugh as the kitchen timer goes off. I hurry to pull the final batch of cookies out, welcoming the heat from the oven. It camouflages the flush of embarrassment. "I'm always smiling."

"No, this is different," Hadlee says, her mouth full. I turn back to find her nibbling the arm off a gingerbread man. She smiles sheepishly when I send her a playful glare. "You're not just smiling—you're happy. Like *really* happy."

"I don't get it," I say, shaking my head. "I'm overall a happy person—at least, I think I am…"

"It's different," she repeats. "I've never seen you this happy, Jay. Like ever—and we've known each other forever. This is more than just happiness."

"What are you talking about?" I laugh, shifting the cookies to a cooling rack before dumping the hot pan into the sink. I flip the cold water on and let it cool the pan as I make sure the cookies turned out.

"I'm talking about that pesky emotion you're terrified to have." Hadlee says, lifting an eyebrow.

Love?

"Don't be silly. I'm not in love with anyone." *Am I?*

"Think about it, Jay." She takes another bite from the cookie and sighs out a moan. "These taste *just* like Mama T's."

"That's because I used her recipe," I say, brushing off the *'love'* comment. *I'm not in love with Alex. That's just ridiculous.* I point toward the living room where the last few Christmas boxes sit, paper strewn about them. "Can you clean that up? Alex and the girls will be here any minute."

"*Alex and the girls,*" she mocks, but I simply smile and roll my eyes. Hadlee takes another bite from the stolen cookie and saunters around the couch. "Sorry I won't be here for movie night with the girls. Tonight was the only night Joey could meet to talk about the booth."

"It's fine, Lee," I say, getting the frosting from the fridge. My hands shake as I fill the piping bags, and I lift my gaze to Hadlee. She stands with her back to me, her oversized sweater hanging from her shoulder as she cleans up the mess of Christmas decorations. I'm glad she can't see the way her words have shaken me.

Memories from the past few weeks with the Hall family fill my mind, and I smile, remembering the look of pure adoration on Alex's face when he watched Maddie skating with me yesterday. He truly loves those girls, and that's why I love him. *Wait, what?* I mentally shake myself. *Love isn't in my plans here. Alex is a friend, nothing more...right?*

"If you don't hear from me by ten, send a search party," Hadlee jokes, pulling her shoes on in the entryway. I blink through the haze of panic flooding me and nod. She waves enthusiastically as she leaves, the door slamming behind her.

Silence settles around me. Sighing out a breath, I steady my shaking hand with the other one and focus on decorating the cookies. I appreciate the peace as I pipe out the little faces, but my mind keeps returning to Alex.

Alex... His face is burned into my memory in a way that singes my very soul. It's the memory of him from that night in the bookshop, eyes rimmed in red, yet set in determination, hair a mess from running his hand through it, lips parted on a breath.

I came back to Harmony with the hope of finding myself again, and somehow, I've landed myself here. Is Hadlee right? Am I throwing myself headfirst into a new relationship where I thought I was creating a friendship? *I don't know.*

I pipe buttons and bowties on the gingerbread men, gnawing on my bottom lip as I go. My relationship with Alex has been nothing short of breathtaking, and I have no desire to ruin that with something as unpredictable as...as *love*.

Falling in love is not in my plans.

Would it be so bad?

No. Not at all.

Loving Alex would be easy.

Too easy.

There's a knock on the door, startling me. My hand slips, and the buttons I was piping turn into a messy squiggle across the gingerbread man's chest. *Dammit.* I blow out a breath and set the icing down. A soft, scattered knock sounds again, and I can't help the laugh that seeps out.

Healing with You

Maddie and Morgan stand on the porch in matching pajamas, boots, and big pink coats. I grin, my heart warming again as I usher them inside. These two girls own my heart, a fact that becomes more and more obvious each time I see them.

"What movie are we watching, Miss Jana?" Maddie asks, already shedding her winter gear. The door clicks shut, and I can feel Alex's presence at my back. His warmth seeps into me, alerting me to how chilled I've become since taking off my sweater while baking.

"I have two you can pick from," I tell Maddie, enjoying the way her face lights in excitement. "Why don't you and Morgan go decide which one we should watch first?"

The squeals of excitement bring goosebumps to my skin, and my smile widens as I watch them rush into the living room. A warm breath caresses the back of my neck, sending heat down my spine and causing my pulse to skyrocket.

"Thanks for having us over, Jana," he says, his voice a low growl near my ear. Butterflies erupt in my stomach. I swallow roughly and bite my lip, trying to ignore the way my body heats at his voice.

"Of course. I love having the girls over," I say, turning around quickly. *Mistake*!

Alex hovers over me, so close that our chests brush. I stumble back a step, and his hand shoots out to rest on my hip, as if he's concerned I'll fall over in my hasty retreat. Breathless and disoriented, I lift my gaze to his. Those golden irises stare into my soul, and everything feels right once more.

"Just the girls?" he asks. There's something in his expression that has me moving closer without thought. My palms rest on his chest as he lifts his free hand to brush a stray curl from my eyes, the pads of his fingers rough as they skim over my cheek.

"No," I hear myself say. Alex's lips twitch in amusement, and I can't look away. My heartbeat is loud in my head, his a firm, steady pace beneath my hands, and suddenly, I'm far too warm.

"Daddy!" Morgan screams from the other side of the room. I let my eyes fall closed, part of me relieved at the interruption. "Maddie won't share the blanket!"

"Get your own, Morg!" Maddie whines. "There's a whole basket right there."

"I should..." Alex trails off, his thumb swiping over my bottom lip. I nod, my tongue darting out subconsciously. He growls low in his throat, and my gut tightens in anticipation. His hands linger for a moment before he drops them and steps around me. "Maddie, please just share with your sister."

"But Daddy!" The argument fades into the background as I stumble back to the kitchen, my hands shaking and my throat dry as a desert.

He was about to kiss me. My stomach twists as I mindlessly start moving the finished cookies onto a plate. I can still feel his fingers on my skin, his breath on my face, his woody scent surrounding me.

If Alex kissed me, everything would change.

Would that be such a bad thing?

No. Not at all.

Loving Alex would be easy.

Halfway through the second movie, the girls are fast asleep.

I collect the plate of crumbs and the mugs of half-finished milk and carry them into the kitchen. Pouring the milk down the drain, I turn on the faucet and let the water warm up. The nerves I've been fighting all night are reaching a pinnacle, but I try to ignore them as I rinse the dishes. From the corner of my eye, I see Alex shift Morgan's head from his lap onto a plush pillow before following me.

I reach for the sponge and douse it in soap before rubbing it roughly against the plate. It gets harder and harder to ignore the tangle of knots in my gut, especially now, with his body heat seeping into my skin.

"I've never seen someone scrub at a dish so ferociously." My scrubbing falters, my eyes flickering to the hot water cascading from the faucet. I hear his sigh and catch him shifting in my peripheral. "Are you alright?"

"I'm fine. Why do you ask?" I say, rinsing the dishes and setting them on the drying rack. When I turn to face him, drying my hands on a dish towel, his brows are raised, and he wears a small smirk. *He's so damn attractive.*

"You've been avoiding me since we got here."

"No, I haven't!" He chuckles at my outburst. I shake my head, smiling sheepishly. "Okay, so maybe I have...a *little* bit."

"Why?" His voice is soft, curious, and when I look up into those soulful eyes, I melt. His fingers brush my cheek, drawing my breath from me and sending my heart galloping away. *This is too damn confusing.* I swallow roughly, turning my face away from him. I move to the island, straightening the leftover cookies just to have something to do with my shaking hands. His voice is low in my ear, full of amusement and something else—something gritty. "Do I make you uncomfortable, Jana?"

"Not at all," I breathe out. Alex spins me to face him, and I have to brace myself against the counter. He's so close, I can almost taste him—the smell of gingerbread cookies and his cedar cologne mingle to overwhelm me.

"I *don't* make you uncomfortable, but you can't meet my eyes."

"It's the opposite, Alex," I say, breathless and confused. "I'm *too* comfortable around you."

"And that's a bad thing?" he asks, his eyes softening a little.

"Yes!" I exhale sharply, pressure building up behind my eyes. *Crying won't help this situation, Jana.* "I can't think straight around you, Alex. It's like my head gets lost and everything goes...fuzzy."

"You make my head all fuzzy too, Jana." He sighs, dropping his head to my neck, his breath hot on my skin. My head gets light, my stomach tightens as I wait in shock for his next move. My mouth dries out as he drags his nose from my collarbone to just below my ear, his breath ragged. "You make me question everything I know, everything I *feel*."

My eyes drop closed as his words heat my skin, and I bite my lip as his hands grip my hips, bringing me flush against him. His fingertips find their way beneath my t-shirt, digging into the supple flesh at my hips. A gasp slips past my lips, and I'm helpless against this feeling.

"Your scent is so *fucking* intoxicating," he continues, inhaling sharply. His lips brush against the skin of my neck, as light as a butterfly's wings. "*You're* intoxicating."

"*Alex...*" Words fail me, and all I can do is grip the cold countertop even tighter.

He groans, the sound vibrating against my pulse. "Say my name like that again, and I'll have to do something about it."

It's a threat—or a promise—and I'm tempted to find out. *But I can't.*

"Alex," I breathe out, somehow finding the strength to pull away. His face is inches from mine, and I fight the urge to lean in and kiss him. His eyes are trained on me, and there's a heat in them that makes my knees buckle. "I-I like you."

"I like you, too, Jana," he says, a devilish smirk playing at his full lips. Lips I wish were back on my skin. My heart skips one beat, then another. His hold on my hips deepens, and he presses his forehead against mine with a soft sigh. "It's taken time for me to accept that, and I can understand if you're not ready."

"It's not that," I say, terrified to burst this bubble I find myself in. How do I explain my concerns to him? "Alex, you've been so amazing—I've loved every moment spent with you and the girls these last few weeks, but..."

"But?"

"You deserve someone who can love you without holding back," I say, turning away. I can just barely see Maddie's head where it rests on the couch arm. "Those little girls? They deserve the world. And I can't give that to you—to any of you."

Alex catches my chin, bringing me to face him once more. I can feel the tears building up, feel them spilling over, even as he smiles sweetly down at me. Gone is the overwhelming heat, replaced by a world of understanding.

"I'm not asking for any of that, Jana," he says. His other hand comes up, cupping my cheek as his thumb traces the tracks left by my tears. Our breath mingles, eyes searching eyes. What I see in his makes my heart stop beating altogether. He dips his head, keeping his eyes trained on mine. "I just want you."

As if to prove his point, he closes the remaining distance between us by claiming my lips with his. His lips are softer than I thought they would be, a perfect contrast to the scratch of his five o'clock shadow. The gentle pressure of his lips sends my mind reeling, and I sag against him as goosebumps ripple over my skin at his touch. He holds me firmly, his body trapping me against the kitchen counter while his fingers tangle in my hair.

I'm breathless, weightless; I feel like I'm flying and falling all at once.

He takes his time, and I savor every caress, every soft flick of his tongue against mine. It's slow, passionate, as if he's memorizing this feeling of our lips pressed together. When he pulls away, our breathing ragged as he rests his forehead on mine, I know my thoughts from earlier were true.

Now that he's kissed me, everything has changed.

CHAPTER SEVENTEEN
ALEX

Nothing feels quite real since I held Jana in my arms and felt her soft curves pressed against my body. Her lips were softer than I'd ever imagined them to be and tasted of sweet vanilla. All I can think of is her intoxicating scent, her deep brown eyes, and the splatter of freckles across her nose. She's branded in my thoughts, my memories, my heart—*everywhere*.

"By the end of the month, you should be—are you even listening?" Benji's voice goes low and angry, and he cusses under his breath. "What's the point of me explaining this shit to you if you're not even gonna pay attention?"

Anger rolls from him in waves, and he slams the pen he's holding roughly against the counter. I'm startled out of my thoughts as the plastic casing shatters beneath the pressure and scatters across the desk.

"Woah, chill, man," I say, lifting my hands in surrender. "You've got my attention now."

"Fucking shit," he mutters under his breath, ignoring me. His brow is furrowed, his jaw set in fury as he collects the larger pieces of the pen casing.

"What's going on, Benji?"

His jaw ticks.

"What's going on is that you're not paying a lick of attention to what I'm trying to tell you about your damn store," he growls. He makes quick work of cleaning up the broken pen, dumping the remains into the trashcan under the desk. "You're fucking distracted."

"So are you," I rebut, crossing my arms over my chest. He scoffs, shaking his head, but doesn't say a word. I take a moment to observe him, taking in his messy curls and the thick beard filling in his jawline. His green eyes have dark circles beneath them, as if he's not been getting enough sleep, and his pupils are dilated. "What the hell is going on with you, Benj?"

"Nothing." He shakes his head and rubs a hand over his face. "Not a damn thing."

"Ben, you know you can talk to me," I say, turning to face him fully. His shoulders are slumped forward, and Harper leans heavily against his leg, quietly supporting him. He doesn't like to talk about it, but I know he still has nightmares about his time overseas—how could he not after everything he went through?

"Do I, Alex?" He sounds depleted, like he's giving up.

"I know I've been distracted lately, but I'm still here for you." He refuses to look at me, and I can see the pain flickering in his face. "I promise, Benj. Always and forever."

"Sure, man." Benji smiles, but it's forced and doesn't reach his eyes. "Always and forever."

The sound of my phone ringing cuts through the silent shop, and Benji shakes his head.

"You get that," he says, straightening the folder of papers in front of him. "I'll just talk to you later about this shit."

"Benj—"

"No, it's cool, man."

I watch him leave; his limp is more pronounced than ever as he descends the stairs with Harper at his side. I make a mental note to corner him later as I pull my phone out of my back pocket and glance at the screen. Leslie's name scrolls across it, and I sigh. Her calls have become more frequent, despite my attempts to ward her off by ignoring every one.

"Leslie, it's not a great time," I say into the phone. A sharp exhale comes through the speaker, my sister-in-law's surprise obvious.

"*Alex.*" Her voice is soft and breathy, and she offers a nervous laugh. "I'm sorry, I just wasn't expecting you to answer."

"Then why call?" I ask, tucking the phone into the crook of my shoulder as I move the cursor across the computer screen. The numbers and graphs make no sense to me, and as they swim in my vision, I begin to wish I had been listening to my brother's explanations.

"I'm in town," she says calmly. "I just thought it might be nice to see you—and the girls, of course."

"I don't know, Les." I shake my head, closing out of the spreadsheets.

"It's been two years, Alex." Her sigh is sad, and it's like a dagger to my heart. Over the phone, she sounds just like Laura. "I was thinking we could get lunch at Sandy's. I know the girls used to love the fries there."

"Yeah, they still do." I pinch the bridge of my nose.

"Does two o'clock sound good?" she asks, her voice hopeful.

"Sure."

I sit in my regular booth near the windows at Sandy's, coffee sitting untouched in front of me as my fingers tap restlessly against my knee. Jana's constant tapping makes sense for the first time since we met. A pit of dread settles in my gut, and no matter how much I try to focus on slowing my breathing, it still feels rushed.

I don't know what possessed me to agree to lunch with Leslie, but here I am, waiting for her to show up. I haven't seen any of Laura's family members since the funeral two years ago, so finding out that she's in town surprised me. Despite her trying to call me every few months over the last two years, I haven't had any contact with Leslie. She's Laura's little sister, a xerox copy of the love of my life, and someone who will no doubt bring up unresolved emotions.

This feeling of anxiety has me on the edge of my seat, ready to bolt from the diner when the bell above the door rings. A slender woman steps inside, her blonde hair falling in waves around her face as she stuffs black sunglasses into her bag. I swallow roughly, past the lump of tears forming in my throat.

Laura.

But it's not my wife.

The woman lifts her head, shaking her hair back and glancing around the diner. Her hazel eyes light on me, and an innocently sweet smile takes over her face.

"Alex, hi," Leslie says, her voice breathier than Laura's was. Her cheeks dimple as she takes the seat across from me and begins to shrug off her coat. "Sorry I'm late. My rental got stuck in a snowbank near the hotel."

"What are you doing in Harmony, Leslie?" I ask. My voice is hoarse and my throat itches with every word. I lean forward, resting my arms on the table. Her eyes are a shade lighter than Laura's, more green than brown, and they dart between mine, searching for something I don't think I can give her.

"I've missed you, Alex," she says softly. *Always so soft, so breathy.* Her hands clasp and unclasp on top of the table as nerves roll in waves from her. "Our parents—well, I know Laura told you about them. When she married you, for the first time,

I felt like a part of something. After Laur... When we lost her, it felt like I was losing my whole family."

"I'm sorry, Les," I say, guilt filling me. "Laura wanted the girls to grow up away from your family, from your parents."

"Why did you cut *me* out?" she asks, her voice full of pain and heartache. She wrings her hands together, pulling roughly at her fingers. "I loved you—all of you. I helped raise your daughters... I don't understand, Alex. I never have."

"Laura wanted a better life for our girls than she had—"

"Laura wanted a better life for me too, Alex."

The tears in her eyes make my heart break all over again. I reach out, placing my hand over hers. The wringing stops, her hands stilling beneath mine. Leslie has always been a slave to her emotions, and I'm surprised by the control she's exerting. She breathes out a long, slow sigh, calming her breathing.

"I'm sorry I cut you out after Laura died," I say, bowing my head. I can't look her in the eyes, can't keep looking at her soft features that look so much like my dead wife's. "I was grieving, and having you around was just too hard."

"I don't—"

"You look just like her, Les."

"*Alex*..." She squeezes my hand, leaning forward over the table.

"I just needed some time."

"It's been two years."

"I know how long it's been, Leslie." I sigh, running a hand through my hair and down my face. Two years is a long time to sit in grief, yet that's what I did. I couldn't pull myself out of it, couldn't find anyone worth fighting my way through. *Until Jana.*

"I know, Alex." Leslie smiles sadly, pulling her hands away from me. She stands and pulls her coat back on. "I've got a meeting I forgot about, but I'll be in town for a few more days. Can we grab dinner tomorrow?"

"Sure." I nod reluctantly.

"And bring the girls this time," she says with a smile, flipping her hair out of her coat collar. "I would love to see them."

"I'll see what I can do."

CHAPTER EIGHTEEN
JANA

I pull on my coat and wave goodbye to Polly and the new guy, Harvey, before hurrying outside. With Mrs. F still stuck in Missoula, Quinn has become overbearing at work, and if I don't hurry, she'll make me stay to clean out the giant mixers. I pull my coat tight around me as I step outside into the chilly winter air.

Hadlee huddles beside the brick wall, bundled in black wool leggings and her black puffer coat. Her sleek hair frames her face, sticking out from under a cream-colored beanie. The little poof on the top wobbles as she bounces in place, trying her best to stay warm.

"What are you doing outside?" I ask, hurrying to her side.

"Like I'm gonna test Q today?" Hadlee says with a dark chuckle. "Better to freeze my cute ass off than face her when she's in boss mode."

"Why *are* you freezing your cute ass off?" I glance up and down the street. "Where's the nice, warm car?"

"The engine overheated—guy said something about the radiator?" she says, linking our arms and pulling me into her side. She's shivering, her shoulder knocking mine as she leads me down the road. "Anyway, it had to be towed—but! I saw Alex's big ass truck in front of Sandy's. I figured we could hitch a ride with him, maybe beg off a few free fries, too."

My face heats at the mention of Alex, and I'm beyond grateful for the nippy air biting at my blushing cheeks. The memory of his hands gripping my hips as his lips devoured mine has been on replay in my mind since it happened.

"What's this?" Hadlee teases, nudging my side. "Are you blushing?"

"No!" I say with a nervous laugh, my cheeks flushing even hotter. "It's just cold out."

"You can say that again," she mutters.

"It's just cold out."

"Shut up," she says, fighting a smile. "No, but really—did something happen last night with the sexy single dad?"

I bite the inside corner of my mouth. By the time Hadlee got home last night, I'd been in bed, pretending to sleep. I still haven't told her about the kiss, and I'm not sure I want to. It was an incredibly intimate and passionate moment, and despite having shared with her in the past, it feels almost too personal.

"Oh my God, something did happen," Hadlee says, yanking me to a stop on the sidewalk. "Did he kiss you?"

"Hadlee—"

"OH MY GOD, HE DID!"

"*Hadlee!*" I hiss, pulling her to the side. I lean against the brick wall in front of the pharmacy. Hadlee giggles like a schoolgirl as an old couple walks past, horrified disgust written plainly across their faces. "Must you always draw so much attention?"

"Alex *kissed* you?"

"I never said that—"

"Your facial expression said it all, Jay."

"Fine, yes, he kissed me." I glance around, my ears ringing from my best friend's excited squeals. Sandy's Diner is directly across the street, and Alex's truck sits parked out front. The thought of seeing him sends my heart into overdrive, and my stomach immediately ties itself into knots. "I-I told him that he makes my head turn on end and go all fuzzy."

"You said that?" Her eyes are wide, and I bite my lip, nodding. It embarrassed me then too. "What did he do?"

"He..." The way he gripped my hips and dragged his nose up my neck plays through my head, and a familiar warmth spreads through me. A shiver takes over my body, but it's not from the cold. "He said I make his head fuzzy too, and that I make him question everything he knows—"

"Oh my God." Hadlee's words are barely a whisper. My cheeks are on fire, and it's all I can do not to hide my face in my hands. "That's so hot. Alex is officially the hottest dad in town."

"Who was the hottest dad before?" I ask, grateful for the distraction.

"Oh, that's easy—" She grins, linking our arms once more and tugging. We cross the street together as I wait for her to continue. "Mr. Delanie."

"Mr. Delanie?" I ask in shock. "Our high school guidance counselor?"

"Oh, please," she says with a laugh. "That hair? And have you seen him jogging in the summer? Gorg bod."

"No, no, I have not," I say, joining her laughter. "Isn't he married?"

"I said he was a hot dad," she says, shaking her head. "I can daydream from afar and not ruin his marriage."

"I suppose you can," I agree as we reach the back of Alex's truck. "As long as you don't go psycho and start thinking your daydreams are real."

"You'd help me bury her body, though, right?"

"Oh, of course."

My laughter dies as I lift my eyes to the diner window. Alex sits in his usual booth, but in place of Maddie and Morgan, there's a gorgeous blonde sitting opposite him. I don't recognize her, but he seems to have an intimate knowledge of her. They lean over the table, heads close and his hand resting over hers as they speak.

"Who the hell is that?" Hadlee voices my question, but there's no one around to answer it. "I'll wring his fucking neck."

"I-I'm sure there's an explanation, Lee," I say softly, watching the woman smile at Alex as she stands up and pulls on a suede jacket. She brushes the hair from his forehead before leaning down to kiss his cheek. My heart shatters.

I tug on Hadlee's arm, ducking behind Alex's big ass truck as the woman steps out of the diner. She glances up and down the street before heading for a small red bug parked a few meters away. Bile bubbles in my esophagus as I watch her climb inside and start the car, driving towards the outskirts of town.

"Why'd you do that?" Hadlee asks, anger radiating from her vibrating body. "I was gonna tear out every strand of her bottle blonde hair and feed it to her."

"There's got to be an explanation," I mumble, my head feeling light. *This is how it starts.*

"There is no good explanation for this."

"Maybe I misinterpreted..."

"Maybe Alex is a good-for-nothing, self-righteous ass—" Hadlee cuts herself off as heavy boots crunch in the snow on the other side of the truck. Alex comes around the front, his eyes on the phone in his hand.

He looks better than I remember, his hair disheveled and cheeks already tinged pink from the cold. I swallow past the lump of tears and betrayal in my throat, trying to focus on something that doesn't remind me of the man who just unknowingly broke my heart.

"Jana?" His voice is like a drug, and I'm drowning in the sound of my name coming from his lips. My brain sputters to a stop as he gets closer, the smell of cedar and oranges flooding my senses. His fingers lift to my cheek, and I flinch involuntarily. "Hey, darling, what's going on?"

"I was wondering the same thing," Hadlee says, venom pouring from her mouth.

"Hadlee's car is in the shop, and we saw your truck over here, so we thought we might hitch a ride—" I cut myself off, realizing I'm rambling. My voice is shaking, and it takes everything in me not to scream. Alex frowns, his brow furrowing as he looks from my glaring friend to me.

"Are you okay?" he asks, resting his hand gently on my shoulder. I look away, refusing to meet that searching amber gaze. "Jana?"

"I'm just tired..." *Tired of the lies. Tired of the betrayal. Tired of everything.*

"Okay," he says, squeezing my shoulder softly. "Do you want me to take you home?"

"Yeah, that would be great."

Alex swings open the driver's side door and holds out his hand. "Climb on up."

Feeling his warm hand wrap around my frozen one, I almost break. Every touch makes me melt, even something as simple as this. I hurry to climb in, sliding across the front seat and settling as far from his space as I can. Hadlee keeps her mouth shut ignoring his offer of help as she climbs into the back.

Healing with You

Once Alex has settled into the driver seat, he reaches across the space between us and hooks his hand under my thigh. My eyes widen as he pulls me firmly into his side before reaching across my lap to fasten my seatbelt. His cologne floods my senses as his amber eyes meet mine. I can feel his warm breath on my face, the hint of coffee lingering.

"I missed you, darling."

His lips brush mine in the softest kiss I've ever experienced, and I feel myself relaxing against him, my eyes fluttering shut. The clearing of a throat startles me, and I push him away. He keeps my hand in his, resting them on his thigh as he starts the truck, a grin of pure happiness etched onto his face.

There's nothing to worry about. Alex wasn't like George—he wouldn't kiss me and say I was enough for him only to turn around and tell someone else the same thing...

Right?

Hadlee's glare is directed at both of us as Alex pulls away from the curb and flips a U-ie. Despite everything, I want to believe there's more to the story—that the scene I saw wasn't what I thought. That Alex wouldn't betray me like the other men I've let into my heart.

I smooth the paper with practiced fingers, folding and taping until the book is wrapped up in a neat little package. Wrapping twine around the book, I loop it through a small note card before tying it securely in a knot.

Despite my best efforts, Hadlee's voice rings in my head. *"You need to confront him about that woman, and then you'll know for sure. Either he's an asshole, just like Jon and George, or he's got a real, honest-to-God reason for meeting with that skank."*

I look up, letting my eyes rest on Alex for a moment. He's tucking bookmarks with the shop's logo under the twine before tying perfect little bows. He's doing a fantastic job, probably from years of practice as a girl dad.

The bookshop is dark except for a few small lamps that light just the area surrounding us. Alex has been just as distracted as me, if not more so, which leaves us in an uncomfortable silence as we work. My stomach is in knots tighter than the ones I'm tying in the twine, and I can't bear the quiet any longer. I clear my throat, the sound echoing loudly through the deserted shop, and Alex lifts his head. Our eyes connect across the stacks of gift-wrapped books, and his lips tilt up as a smile overtakes his face. He sets down the book he was working on and scoots closer to me on the floor.

"How was your day?" I ask hesitantly, wondering if he'll mention the woman on his own or if I'll have to outright ask him. He drapes his arm over my shoulders and tangles his fingers into my hair. I swallow past the lump in my throat, trying not to get distracted by the warmth of his firm body.

"Pretty average," he says, his fingers rubbing gently against my scalp. I sigh and find myself relaxing into his side despite myself. "Maddie had ballet, and Morgan spent the afternoon with Benji."

"That must've been nice—having an afternoon free, I mean?"

"Sure, I guess," he says, his breath warm on my temple, his voice low in my ear. I pick up the black pen and start writing a basic description of the romcom inside on the notecard. I focus on forming the letters instead of the soft circular motions he makes with his fingers on my scalp.

"Did you do anything fun?"

"Not really," he says, sounding tired. "After I dropped you home, I had to run to the store to get Maddie's Christmas present. She's been begging for that model train with the lights that blows steam."

"Did you find one?" I ask, disappointed he skipped over the lunch he had before he saw me. I set the book on top of the pile in front of me. There's only another six or seven left to wrap, but my energy has disappeared.

"Yeah, finally." When I glance at him, his eyes are distant, and he mindlessly twirls a strand of my dark hair around his finger. "I had to drive out to Windham to get it, though."

"That's quite the drive," I say softly, tapping the pen against the table in a soft rhythm. He offers a noncommittal hum, still distracted. I nibble on the cuticle of my thumb, hating how distant he's being. *George started acting like this a few months before I found him with Jessica.* "Are you okay, Alex?"

"What?" He turns to me, blinking the fog from his eyes. I rest my hand on my knee, tapping, trying to ease this aching anxiety bubbling in my chest. *This can't be happening. Not again.*

"Are you okay?" I ask again, my voice small.

"Yeah, of course," he says, shaking his head a little as he smiles at me. He pulls me closer, pressing a soft kiss to my forehead. "Just a little distracted. Do you want a ride home?"

The undeniable press of tears builds behind my eyes, and I mentally curse myself for being such an emotional baby. Nodding, I struggle to my feet, putting as much distance between us as I possibly can. "Yeah, it's, um, it's getting l-late."

"Jana, is everything okay?" Alex asks, following behind me as I gather my coat and bag, suddenly paying much closer attention than he previously was. I feel him at my back as I straighten, the tears threatening to fall at any moment. I blink, begging them to disappear, but with no such luck. Alex moves around me as the first ones fall, and even through the salt water, I can see the concern wash over his expression. "Why are you crying?"

"Oh my God, I'm sorry," I say, wiping away the traitorous tears. This is not how this was supposed to play out. I was going to wait and see if he brought her up, but I couldn't control these damn waterworks.

"Sorry?" Alex's expression morphs from concern to confusion. He cups my cheek, his thumb dragging through the path of tears as he studies my face. "Never apologize for having feelings, darling."

Even now, he's better than either of my cheating exes.

"I-I saw you." My cheeks flush as I get more worked up. He still looks confused, his amber eyes holding nothing but worry. I'm sure I look ridiculous, standing before him in my leggings and college sweater, my hair a mess and my face blotchy from the tears. Flashbacks from years ago come back in full force, of Jon laughing in my face when I confronted him about the affair with his TA. "I saw you with the blonde woman."

Understanding floods his countenance, and he sets his jaw.

"At the diner." It's not a question. He knows exactly what I'm talking about, and I'm grateful he has the decency to own up to it. "And it looked like we were on a date?"

"Alex, I—"

"No, it's okay," he says, a soft, sad smile appearing. He caresses my cheek, his eyes glimmering with an unspoken emotion. "I meant what I said, Jana. I just want you—*no* one and *nothing* else. And I'm willing to wait—*forever* if I have to."

My heart does a little flop, my stomach tightening as new tears build in my lashes. He stands so close, I can see the whisper of gray in his beard, the wrinkles in the corners of his eyes. This isn't a boy, unsure of what he wants. This is a man; one who's experienced a love and loss so profound, it would break my heart. This is a man who knows *exactly* what he wants.

His arms slip around my waist, trapping my hands against his chest as he pulls me firmly against him. He dips his head, allowing our noses to bump together gently, our lips a hairsbreadth apart. I can smell the candy cane he was nibbling earlier on his breath and feel the scratch of his beard against my cheek, all my senses working together to bring me to the edge of sanity.

When his lips touch mine, it's like I'm frozen in time. Warmth seeps into me at his touch, and I allow my eyes to drift shut. He holds me like I'm fragile, as though I'll break if he puts too much pressure on me. It's me who moves to deepen the kiss, sliding my hands to his neck and tangling my fingers in his hair as my tongue swipes over his lips. When they part, slanting over mine, I feel like I'm falling, endlessly.

By the time we pull apart, my tears have dried, and my heart hurts a little less. Alex presses soft kisses to my lips and jaw, his fingers finding mine and lacing them together as he rests his forehead against mine. We stand there, a heated silence between us. His eyes are closed, but even so, I can see a myriad of emotions flicker across his face.

"The blonde woman you saw at the diner." Alex pauses and inhales sharply. His brows furrow, the muscle in his jaw jumping. "She's Laura's little sister—my sister-in-law."

"Oh." It's all I can manage as nerves begin bubbling in my gut again. *Sister-in-law?* There was so much unspoken chemistry between them; there's no way that's all it was.

"I promise, Jana," he says, staring into my eyes. There's something there that makes me want to trust him, to believe everything he says. He kisses me deeply, fiercely. "You've got nothing to worry about."

Don't I? My gut twists. The shared loss is one thing, but the uncanny resemblance to his wife—how am I supposed to believe she won't tempt him? That those emotions won't transfer?

"Come on, I'll take you home."

I allow him to wrap his arm around my shoulders and lead me to the door. As we step outside, fresh snow falling, I glance up and down the street while he locks the door. I inhale, the icy air burning down my throat before I exhale a shuddering breath. *Nothing to worry about.* I force a smile as he turns around.

"Are you really not going to decorate the store for Christmas?" I ask playfully, letting my fears sink into the dark recesses of my mind. Alex laughs, pulling me into his side as we walk toward his truck.

"Who knows." He shrugs, grinning happily as he helps me step up into the truck. "You might convince me yet, darling."

CHAPTER NINETEEN
ALEX

"I'll be back to pick you up after, Bug," I tell Morgan, giving her one last hug before she runs off to join the other kids gathering in the center of the room. She's wearing one of Maddie's old leotards and pink leggings. This pop-up tumbling class put on by the gymnastics coach was a lifesaver in the afternoons, and I'm glad Morgan is finally willing to stay by herself.

I watch for another moment, making sure she doesn't need me before I step outside. The air is cold, and I zip my jacket against the gentle breeze that's picking up. It flings the powder like snow up into the air and into my face.

I glance up and down the street, surprised by how dead it is. Sure, it's the middle of the day, but with the holiday festival just around the corner, I was sure it would be utter chaos on Main Street. Yet, it's peaceful, the bright snow dampening the sound of the few cars that do pass through.

Tucking my hands into my jacket pockets, I make my way down the sidewalk, heading for Sandy's Diner. I'm a few minutes late, but I know Jana won't mind. When I asked her to meet me for lunch, she'd smiled that shy, dimpled grin that takes my breath away and agreed.

I'm glad for it too.

Ever since I met with Leslie, the light in Jana's eyes had dimmed significantly. I hate seeing her so vulnerable, so distraught, and the utter heartbreak and pain that lingers in her gaze now makes me want to kill whoever caused that distrust to grow in her.

After our talk the other night, I skipped dinner with Leslie. It felt wrong to meet with her after Jana voiced her concerns. Hurting her is the last thing I want to do, and despite knowing there is nothing between Leslie and me, it wasn't something I was willing to test.

Jana is *everything*.

I love her.

I pause, my steps faltering as the thought comes. Warmth blooms in my chest, a slow burn that seeps through me until I'm no longer cold at all. For the first time in two years, my head and my heart are on the same page.

I love Jana—with everything left in me.

When Laura passed, I never thought I would feel this way about another person again, yet here I am, desperate for my beautiful, curvy brunette.

"Alex?"

I turn my head at the sound of Leslie's voice, surprised to find her blocking my path forward. She's disheveled, her blonde hair a mess beneath a hastily placed cap, her mascara smudged. There's a crazed look in her red-rimmed eyes, and as I watch, she sways on her feet.

"Les, what's going on?"

"Y-you haven't been answering my c-calls," she says, her words stuttered. My heart aches seeing her like this, but before I can say anything, she steps forward, wringing her hands as she continues. "I-I need to talk to...to you."

"Leslie, I think you should go back to the hotel," I say, patting her shoulder. The moment my hand touches her, she sags against me, her eyes glossing over.

"N-no, I need to get this..." Her voice shakes. "I need to get this o-out."

My brow furrows, and I lead her to the brick wall, helping her lean against it. Her clothes reek of alcohol and vomit, and now that we're standing so close, I can see the tracks of dried tears left behind on her ruddy cheeks.

"You broke your sobriety." It's a statement, not a question. She turns her head away in shame, tears crowding her lower lashes. She's shaking like a leaf—whether from the cold or her nerves, I'm not sure. "Les, what happened?"

"Laura died," she says, her voice breaking. "My sister *died*, and I couldn't do it anymore. I had nothing—no one to care."

Guilt flares to life at her words and I clench my jaw, looking down. Amidst my own grieving, I'd left this woman alone in her time of need. Laura had spent a year helping Leslie get sober. She was there through it all, and I should've known losing her would leave Leslie in a vulnerable place.

"I should've been there."

"It's not your f-fault, Alex," she says softly, turning to face me. "It was my choice to drink, and I…I tried to get sober again. I promise you, I tried, but it's like I'm stuck in quicksand, and every move I make sucks me right back in."

"Do you have a sponsor?" I ask. I remember a phone call between Laura and Leslie, the discussion of getting her a sponsor once she moved back to New York.

"Of course," she says, her lips turning down. "But he's been away. I thought…I thought seeing you and the girls—"

"You thought it would help?"

"You were there when Laura helped me," Leslie says. She bites her thumbnail, looking everywhere but at me. "You were my safe space, Alex."

"Leslie—"

"Alex, please…" She pauses, taking a deep breath before she lifts her eyes to mine. There's a determination there that seems to be fueled by the alcohol still pumping through her system. "I can't pretend with you—I don't want to."

"What are you talking about, Les?"

"I love you, Alex." Her voice is soft, her hazel eyes full of nerves and a glimmer of hope. "I've loved you for ten years, but I was too afraid to tell you." A sob slips out, tears spilling over. "I thought...I thought I could make these feelings go away when you married Laura, but..." She shakes her head. "You plagued my mind. That's why I left—being here, sleeping one room away from you and never being anything more than your sister-in-law—I couldn't take it anymore."

Her words throw me off, and I stumble back a step.

"Alex, I know you loved my sister," she continues. "And I know you're still grieving her, but I can't pretend like I don't have feelings for you anymore."

"Leslie..." I clear my throat, trying to make sense of what's happening. "You're drunk. We should get you back to the hotel so you can sleep it off."

"No, I'm not drunk, just...just a little hungover," she admits. "I've just been too afraid to say any of this, and now...now I'm not. I needed to tell you, to get it out of my head and just...be honest."

"Leslie, you're a beautiful woman," I say softly, running my hand through my hair. "And you've got a big heart, but..."

I love Jana.

"Alex, wait," she says, stepping closer to me and pressing a finger against my lips. Her eyes dart between mine, searching for something. I don't know what she sees there, but she drops her hand and leans her cheek against my chest. I feel her sigh deeply, and then her arms are around me in a hug. "I'm sorry. I never should've come back."

"Les—"

"You don't have to say it, Alex," she says softly. She lifts her head and looks up at me, a small, sad smile on her lips. "I can see it written on your face. You're in love."

"I'm sorry, Les."

I can't help but wrap my arms around her, pulling her into a tight hug. I've always seen her as a little sister, exactly like Carlee. She deserves better than this, but there's nothing I can do now except offer her comfort.

We stand there for a moment more before Leslie pulls back, laughing lightly and wiping tears with the sleeve of her suede jacket. "Do you remember when we met, Alex?"

I blow out a breath, shoving my hands into my pockets as I glance out at the snow-covered street. "That first Thanksgiving I came home with Laura, right?"

"No." I swing my gaze back to her, surprised. She smiles sadly. "We met before that. In the library at Brown."

"What?" I wrack my brain, trying to remember the encounter she's talking about, to no avail.

"You were looking for Dostoevsky's *Crime and Punishment* for your English Lit class," she says. Her eyes are full of disappointment, and she looks away before I can see more tears fall. "I was sitting at a table in the back corner, studying for my history midterm. You came up to me with that damn smile, and I was hooked. I helped you find the book and you asked for my number, but you never called me. I guess we know why."

She laughs again, and my shoulders slump. I have no recollection of this meeting.

"Looks like I missed my shot again," she says.

"Leslie—"

"Don't, Alex," she says, shaking her head. "I don't want pity, okay? I'm happy for you, truly. I hope everything works out with this one."

"You'll find someone," I say in a last-ditch effort to ease my guilt. She bites her bottom lip and nods. "You're smart and funny—not to mention, you're gorgeous."

A sharp, surprised laugh rips from her, the first real smile pulling at her lips. "I really am happy for you, Alex. You deserve love in your life."

"So do you, Leslie." She looks away, tears welling on her waterline. "You deserve someone who loves you ferociously. Please don't settle, okay?"

Leslie stares hard at me, stepping closer after a moment. She lifts her hand, brushing the hair from my forehead. She pushes up on her tiptoes, and I think she's going to kiss my cheek. I'm surprised when her mouth claims mine instead in a soft kiss. Her lips are cold against mine, nothing like Jana's warm and full lips. I jerk away, shock rushing through my system. Leslie simply smiles that sad smile.

"I wasn't settling, Alex."

CHAPTER TWENTY
JANA

The diner buzzes around me, full of life and laughter. I sit at Alex's usual booth, picking apart a paper napkin as I wait for him to appear. My phone lights up on the table, and I glance at the notification: ***hadeebear sent you a video***. I clench my jaw, my teeth grinding as I read the time. Alex is twenty minutes late.

I abandon the napkin for my phone, pulling up the rest of the notifications. There are a few more funny videos from Hadlee and Wren in our group chat, a weather update, and a spam email. Nothing from the man I'm supposed to be meeting.

When I got his text this morning, asking to meet him for lunch, I'd been ecstatic. The fear of history repeating itself slowly slipped away, and I dolled myself up more than I have in months. Sitting here now, alone, I can't help but let the nagging voice slip back to the forefront of my mind.

This is how it starts.

I shake my head, huffing out a sigh. *He's just late. It's nothing to worry about.*

I remember him telling me he had to drop Morgan off at a tumbling class before he could head over. Maybe she didn't want him to leave right away, and he just left his phone in the truck. *Yeah, that's it.*

I nibble on my bottom lip, my fingers going back to the napkin in front of me. Sandy brings me another hot chocolate, a sweet smile on her lips.

"Are you sure you don't wanna order some food, sweetheart?" she asks. "You look a little pale."

My hand flies to my cheek, and I shake my head, forcing a smile. "No, that's okay. I'm waiting for Alex."

"Looks like he's got his hands full," she replies, lifting her brows and jutting her chin toward the window. "I'll just get you some fries while you wait."

She walks away as my eyes fly to the window. The sun reflects brightly off the snow, and I have to squint a little to see the man standing on the opposite sidewalk. My heart sinks as my anxious thoughts seem to be laughing at me. Alex is standing in front of the pharmacy with his sister-in-law.

They stand opposite each other, their eyes locked, and when she laughs...

Pain rips through my heart as she steps even closer to him, cupping his jaw in her palm and rising on her tiptoes. *Push her away.* I can't tear my gaze from them. *Please, Alex. Push her away.* Her lips connect with his in a soft kiss, and even though I've closed my eyes, I can still see the image burned into the back of my eyelids.

My chest feels tight, and tears begin to fall of their own accord as I gather my things. My coat goes on, followed by my winter hat, before I fish some cash out of my bag. I drop the bills on the table for my hot chocolate before rushing out of Sandy's Diner. I keep my eyes trained on the icy ground, blinking through the tears that refuse to go away.

I never should've come back to Harmony.

The pain in my chest feels like someone stabbed me through with a hot poker, and no matter how much I try, I can't make it go away. I take in a shuddering breath in, trying to find some sense of calm in the storm that rages through me.

"*Jana!*"

Alex's voice shatters through my panic, and my steps falter. The memory of Jon laughing in my face, of George's smirk as he continued to fuck Jessica over my couch, fill my head. *No. I will not take it again.* I force my feet to keep moving, hating the sting of cold against my tear-stained cheeks.

"Jana, please—"

"No!" I bite out, hating how much I've let him hurt me. "I can't do this, Alex."

"Jana, I swear, nothing happened."

"Don't *fucking* lie to me," I say, spinning around to face him. He skids to a halt, pure guilt written across his handsome face. I'm haunted by him. Even now, when I hate him with every fiber of my being, I can't deny that. "I know what I saw, and I refuse to let you gaslight me."

"I would never gaslight you, darling." I flinch at the endearment that once made my heart beat wildly in my chest. Now all it gets is a small flutter from the damaged organ.

"You *kissed* her, Alex!" The words hang in the air between us and my last defenses break as reality settles in. "I...I *trusted* you. I thought you were different than the others, but you're not."

"*Jana*..." His voice breaks on the word, and I can see his heart breaking. He takes a step, trying to close the distance between us, but I step backward. His amber eyes fill with tears, and it takes everything in me to stand my ground.

"I can't do this anymore, Alex."

"I swear, Jana," he says softly. "I swear, it was nothing. *She* kissed *me*—"

"You let her, Alex," I reply, hating that more tears fall. "You never should've put yourself in that position, and you know it. Something in you wanted it—wanted her. And my heart can't afford that kind of collateral damage."

"Jana—"

"No." I shake my head and take another step away from him. "I have to trust myself now, because if I don't...if I don't, then I'll be stuck in the same heartbreaking cycle as always."

"I love you, Jana."

I'd wanted to hear those words from him, but now that they've come, it only breaks my heart more. A sob breaks through, and I cover my mouth with a hand, stumbling backward. He tries to reach for me again, tears running down his own cheeks, but I know if I let him touch me, I'll never follow through with leaving him. Instead, I straighten my shoulders and turn around, leaving him alone in the middle of the street.

"Goodbye, Alex."

Tissues are scattered across the floor, and I'm curled up on the couch, a blanket wrapped securely around my body. *It's a Wonderful Life* plays on the TV for the second time tonight, and I stare blankly at the screen as George Bailey screams into the void of the river.

"Jay?" Hadlee's voice is soft, concern ringing through the space between us. I blink through the new tears building up, hating that I've spent the entire afternoon crying over another man. *But he wasn't just another man.* "Oh, honey."

"What happened, Jan?" Quinn asks softly, sitting by my feet. I sniffle, reaching for another tissue as the tears spill over. Hadlee crouches in front of me, effectively blocking the screen from my view and forcing me to meet her gaze.

"You were right," I say, trying to keep the tears at bay. I'm so sick of crying, but the tears refuse to stop falling. "I just feel so *stupid*, Lee."

"Right about what?" Quinn asks.

"*Alex*." My voice breaks. My chest aches, and it feels like someone spent the day stomping on my heart.

"I don't want to be right about this, Jay," Hadlee says, pushing my dark curls away from my face.

"He kissed her."

"That good-for-nothing, two-timing—" Quinn's angry rant is cut off by a sharp glare from Hadlee. She settles with a huff, placing a hand on my knee. "How did you get home?"

"I walked."

"That's like a twenty-minute walk," Hadlee says with a frown. Her brows furrow, and I shrug. Twenty minutes is nothing when compared to this pain in my heart. "You should've come to the salon, hon; I could've at least given you a ride home, so you didn't freeze your ass off."

I shake my head. "I couldn't—I needed time."

"That's understandable."

"How did you find out?" Quinn asks, barely keeping her voice level. I flick my eyes to her. Anger rolls off her in waves, and I'm grateful to have her on my side. I would hate to incur the wrath of the petty redhead.

"We were supposed to meet for lunch," I say. More tears catch on my lashes, and I grit my teeth. I hate how easily the tears come for him. The memory of their kiss is burned into my head, and it's all I see when I close my eyes. "He was late, and..." I bite my cheek, trying to hold back the sob sitting in my chest. "I saw them across the street."

Hadlee holds out a fresh tissue, and I take it, wiping the tears and snot from my face. "Does he know you know?"

"Yeah."

His tearful confession will haunt me for the rest of my life. I push myself into a seated position, struggling to breathe with a tear-stuffed nose. I know this is my own fault; I never should've gotten involved with him in the first place. Now my heart has shattered, and I'm left in pieces without him.

"Hey, it's okay."

I shake my head. "H-he...he came after me."

No one's ever come after me.

"What happened then?" Quinn asks in a whisper.

"I told him I saw the kiss, and he..." I pause to blow my nose, wiping tears with my sleeve. "He tried to explain, but I just...I told him I can't do this again."

The girls are silent as another sob wracks through my body. My body aches, a physical manifestation of my breaking heart. Every memory I have of Alex has been playing on repeat in my mind since I left him standing in the street, and each one hurts more than the last. I curl in on myself, as if that will keep my broken pieces in place.

"You did the right thing, Jan," Quinn says softly, squeezing herself into the space beside me and wrapping her arm around my shoulders. Hadlee nods, smoothing back my hair in the same way my mom used to when I was upset. "Breaking things off before you got more invested."

I lean my head on Quinn's shoulder, not even bothering to fight the sob that rips through me this time. "Then why does it feel like my heart's been ripped from my chest?"

"Oh, honey."

"I think I really love him," I say, dashing tears away as they try to blur my vision again. "I saw a life with him and the girls, and now…now I feel so lost and broken."

"I know," Hadlee says, squeezing my hand.

Quinn rests her head on mine, her grip on me tightening. "It'll get easier with time, Jan."

"It's n-never hurt this b-bad before," I cry, hiccuping on every other breath as they crowd me, offering their love and support. "I d-don't know h-how I'm going to h-heal from this o-one."

CHAPTER TWENTY-ONE
ALEX

My fist connects with the wall as I let out a scream of frustration. Everything has fallen apart, and it's nobody's fault but mine. *God, I'm a fucking idiot!*

Seeing Jana rush from the diner as Leslie walked away, I knew. She saw the kiss. Nothing I say or do can ever erase that from her head—or her heart. Every tear that fell from her eyes broke me in ways I wasn't ready for—I'm not sure I'll ever be ready for that, actually. I never thought I could love someone as much as I love Jana, and the fact that I fucked it up in a matter of seconds destroys me.

"Daddy, why are you crying?" Morgan asks, pulling on the hem of my t-shirt. I look down, finding both of my daughters watching me with concerned expressions. *How am I supposed to tell them that Jana and I...*

"Oh, I'm just having a hard day, Bug," I reply. She tilts her head, studying me in a way that's far too similar to Jana. My heart breaks a little more.

"Do you need a hug?" She holds her arms out wide, and I sink to my knees in front of her. Her little arms wrap around my neck, squeezing like a vice grip as I wrap her in a tender hug. Pressure builds behind my eyes and my vision blurs with tears as she mumbles softly in my ear, "It's okay, Daddy. Tomorrow will be better."

I pull away and place a soft kiss on her forehead. Morgan giggles as my beard scratches her baby-soft skin, and I smile lightly at her. "Thanks, Bug."

"Daddy, can Jana come over and make cookies with us?" Maddie asks. My eyes flicker to where my seven-year-old stands, a book held tightly in her arms.

"Oh, um...I don't know, Mads." My mind races to find an excuse, because I still have no idea how to tell them why Jana won't be coming over. "I've got to run an errand, but I can see if Wren can come babysit. Does that sound good?"

"Okay," she sighs dejectedly. "But can Jana come over tomorrow?"

"We'll see, honey."

Maddie frowns but doesn't fight Morgan when she urges her to run back to their bedroom to play Barbies. I watch them run down the hallway, grateful their hearts are still intact. *If I have any say in it, they'll stay that way.* Pulling my phone out, I dial Wren's number and press the device to my ear. It goes directly to voicemail, and I grit my teeth as a new text message appears a second later.

WREN
I'm on her side, Alex.

You need to fix this.

ME
What do you think I'm trying to do?

try harder.

That's what I get for falling in love with my babysitter's best friend.

This time, I dial Benji.

He answers on the first ring. "Hello?"

"Benj, I fucked up."

"I heard," he says. Harper yips on his end of the call, and he chuckles lightly at her. *"Hush now. I'm talking to Alex."*

"What does that mean?" I ask, pinching the bridge of my nose.

"I was with Wren when she got Quinn's call," he explains. I can hear paper rustling and then silence. "So, what are you gonna do?"

"I don't know what to do, Ben," I admit. The only thing on my mind is finding Jana and convincing her that what I feel for her isn't just a schoolboy crush. This heartache proves that if nothing else. "I need to see her—to talk to her."

"Good luck with that," he says with a laugh. "I dropped Wren off at Hadlee's, and those girls are fuming. I wouldn't willingly walk into that house."

"Can you come watch my girls?" I ask. "I've kind of lost my babysitter, too."

"As long as I'm not the one walking into the chaos that is Quinn Shields and Hadlee Scott."

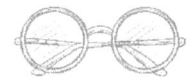

The little house is lit up with Christmas lights, a deceptively calm exterior to the storm that is sure to await me inside. I spent the entire drive here trying to come up with something—anything—to say to Jana, but everything I thought up came out sounding like an excuse. She deserves better than a man making excuses.

She deserves the world—no, more. She deserves this galaxy and the next.

My heart is in my throat as I shut off the truck and climb out, letting my feet trace the familiar pathway through the snow to the front door. I lift my hand to knock but pause. *She hates me, and rightfully so.* It hurts to know the truth, but I've hurt her more than her hating me ever could.

The thought of letting her go on hating me flickers across my mind. To never hold her again, never feel her heart race or her breath stutter when I lean in to kiss her, never get to call her mine—anger flares through me, and I pound my fist against the door. I will never let that happen. Whatever it takes, I'll do it. I can't lose Jana.

My hands grip the doorframe, every second feeling like a lifetime. I drop my head, searching the snow packed beneath my feet for some kind of answer to my problems. *How am I supposed to convince Jana that I love her?*

The door swings open, Hadlee's harsh glare directed at me. Her green eyes glare daggers into my skull, and I fight the urge to hold my hands up in surrender. "You shouldn't be here."

"I need to talk to Jana."

"Yeah, there's no way in hell that's happening." She stands her ground, arms crossed over her chest. I sigh, clenching and unclenching my jaw. There's a part of me that hates her for standing between me and the woman I love, but a bigger part, the rational part, is grateful Jana has such amazing friends.

"Please, Hadlee," I say softly. The tears are back, and I flinch as the first one falls, creating a path down my cheek into my beard. "I need to see her."

"Well, she doesn't want to see you, Alex," she says, her voice firm. I drop my head again, but this time, the snow blurs in my vision. Hot, angry tears slip out, melting the snow they land on and making it hard for me to focus. I close my eyes against the onslaught of pain and heartache, knowing the only cure to this feeling is the woman hidden inside.

Taking a shuddering breath, I lift my head and meet Hadlee's calculating gaze once more. "Tell her...tell her I love her. And I'm not giving up on us. Tell her...I'm willing to wait forever if that's what it takes. She owns my heart. Forever and always."

CHAPTER TWENTY-TWO
ALEX

Benji had the girls asleep by the time I got home. Now, we sit in silence, wallowing in our own thoughts. My hands grip the piano bench tightly, my eyes focused on the black and ivory keys like they've been for the last twenty minutes. Jana's tear-strewn face is burned into my mind, and every time I close my eyes, it's all I can see. Her words, bit out on tears, echo in my head. *"I can't do this anymore, Alex."*

I slam the piano shut, the keys rattling against each other with the force of it.

"Shit, what did that piano ever do to you, Lexi?" Benji asks from his spot across the room.

I push off the bench, and it tumbles back, landing on its side.

"I'm not just gonna give up!" I yell, the anger and pain boiling over. "I can't lose her now. I just can't, Ben. I need her."

"Okay, so what are you gonna do?" he asks, leaning forward. His elbows rest on his knees, his hands clasped as he looks up at me expectantly.

"That's a good fucking question."

Benji chuckles, shaking his head. "Alex, this is a huge mess. You've got to fix it or you *will* lose her."

"Don't you think I know that?" I sigh, pacing back and forth in front of the Christmas tree. It's yet another reminder of Jana and the impact she's had on my life. An unbidden memory floods my mind—her shy smile as we bumped into each other after she almost spilled hot chocolate all over me. "She's *everything*, Benj. I can't imagine my life without her."

"So prove it to her, Alex," Benji says, as if it's that simple.

"How?" I groan, sinking into the couch and dropping my head into my hands. "Her friends are running interference and won't let me near her."

"You need to get them on your side."

"No shit," I say, sending him a glare. "How am I supposed to do that?"

"I can help with Wren," he says. "But you'll need a plan beforehand. Those girls are fiercely loyal to each other; you can't just expect to waltz in there, say sorry, and have them swoon."

"I would never."

I stare at the Christmas tree, the twinkling lights having a calming effect on my mind.

"You need a grand gesture—you know." Benji waves his hand, in a circular motion. "Like in those stupid romcoms Carlee always made us watch."

A grand gesture. Something to show Jana just how much she's changed me in the short time we've been together—to prove I love her and that she means everything to me.

Something niggles at the back of my mind. *I couldn't help but notice you haven't decorated the storefront for Christmas.*

Our first meeting plays out in my mind like a comical dream as a plan begins to form.

"I think I've got an idea, but I'm gonna need your help to get Jana's friends on my side."

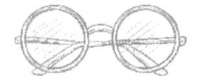

I follow Benji into the bakery, noting the way Harper presses into his leg as he walks. I've noticed her additional attention lately and wonder silently if his injury is acting up. He never talks about the injury or his experience receiving it. I don't know the story, and as much as I've tried to get him to open up to me, I don't think I ever will.

"Aww, hi, pretty girl," Quinn coos from behind the counter, smiling down at Harper as they approach. Her eyes dart to Benji. "I know she's working, but would you like a treat for her?"

"I'm sure she'd love that, Quinn," he replies with an easy grin. I step up beside my brother, and Quinn's gaze flickers to me. The warmth within disappears instantaneously, a look of pure hatred taking its place.

"Get out."

"Quinn, I just want to see her."

"I don't give a shit, Alex," she spits, crossing her arms. "Get out. Now."

"Quinn, hear him out—" Benji shuts his mouth when her death glare is turned on him.

"There's nothing he can say that will fix this," she says, handing him a biscuit for Harper. "Now, get out before I call the Sheriff for harassment."

I raise my hands in surrender and back away from the counter. It's obvious Quinn is going to be the toughest one to get through to. A flash of dark curls catches my attention, and I look at the swinging kitchen door. *She's listening in.*

"Just tell her I'm sorry," I say, loud enough it should carry to my eavesdropping darling. "I'm going to fix this and prove that I love her."

"That's great, Romeo." Quinn rolls her eyes. "Now, get the fuck out."

I sigh but let Benji usher me out. The small bell chirps as the door swings open then shut. Glancing up and down the street, I pull my jacket tighter around my body. Benji crouches beside me and offers Harper the treat, scratching her ears as she chomps away at the little biscuit.

"Now what?"

"Well, Wren said she was getting her hair done today," he says, looking in the direction of the salon from his position on his knees. "We can corner her and Hadlee, get them to listen to your side of the story. Maybe you can convince them to help you win Jana back."

I nod. My whole plan hinges on getting Jana's friends to help me, and if I can't...well, I don't want to think about it. We begin walking toward the salon, Harper trotting along happily between us. I'm glad the girls are in their final classes today, making it easy to keep their little hearts intact until I can fix things with Jana.

"Do you think we can get them to listen?"

"I dunno about Hadlee, but Wren will at least listen," Benji says, ruffling his hair with his free hand. Harper's leash is secured around the other one, a loose lead, simply there for show. He shifts to avoid an older couple walking down the street, giving them a friendly smile. My face is screwed into its usual furrowed brow.

"I hope so," I say, stuffing my hands into the pockets of my coat. The last few days without Jana's sweet smile have wreaked havoc on my heart, and my head. My good morning texts have been left unanswered, the flowers I hand-delivered to her house were left out in the snow, and my attempt at baking oatmeal chocolate chip cookies was a burnt reminder lingering in my kitchen. "I need her, Benj."

"So you've said."

"Come on," I say, frowning. "What if you lost Wren? If she stopped trusting you, you'd be a wreck."

"Yeah, but there's no fucking chance of that," he says, raising an eyebrow. "I'd never be stupid enough to hurt Wren like this."

"You're stupid enough not to tell her how you really feel," I reply bitterly. His brow furrows, the muscles in his jaw twitching as he grits his teeth.

"Sure, make *me* hate you too," Benji says, picking up his pace. "It's not like I'm the only person still on your side."

"Shit, Benj," I sigh, grabbing his arm. "I'm sorry, I didn't mean it."

"Wren has so much on her plate right now, she doesn't need me to ruin the only thing that's easy for her." His shoulders slump a little, and he glances up at the mountain that shades our town. "I'm okay just being her friend right now. As long as I've got her in my life, I don't need anything more."

We continue walking in silence, each of us consumed by our own thoughts. Sadness wars with frustration in my gut, and I rub a hand over my face. Leslie's confession, while slightly flattering, was the last thing I'd expected when she approached me on the street. I'd been so wrapped up in Jana—and my feelings for her—I hadn't been paying attention to my surroundings.

Much like now.

I crash into Benji's back as he stops in front of Casey's Cuts.

"Maybe you should let me do the talking?" he suggests with a playful smirk.

"Let's just see if they'll even let us in," I reply, pushing past him and pushing open the door.

There's a low hum of chatter throughout the salon that mingles with the classic rock playing softly over the speakers. I glance around, looking for a specific brunette. She stands near the back wall, mid-laugh when she catches sight of me. I stalk past the protesting receptionist, heading directly for my goal.

"Jana's not here," Hadlee says, a frown pulling at her perfectly glossed lips.

"That's fine," I say, glancing between her and the blonde in her chair. Wren wears a black cape over her clothes, her hair a mess of tangles and what looks like tin foil. "I was actually looking for you two."

"Us?" Wren says, surprise written across her face. Her mismatched eyes flicker to something over my shoulder, and her cheeks flush a deep shade of pink. "Benji, hi."

It's barely a squeak, but my brother smiles brightly back at her. "Hey, little bird."

"You're not gonna get anything from us, if that's your plan," Hadlee says, ignoring her friend's obvious reaction to Benji. "You're a fucking idiot, Alex. She's been crying nonstop since that kiss, and it's your fault."

"I swear, that kiss was never supposed to happen," I say, rubbing a hand over my face. "Leslie cornered me, and I couldn't just leave her there in her condition. She confessed a ten-year crush and—"

"*Right.*" She drags the word out, rolling her eyes as she crosses her arms. She taps a slow rhythm on her forearm with nails that look like they could tear out a throat, watching me with a raised eyebrow. "Because you're just *that damn charming.*"

"I don't go around kissing people, Hadlee."

"It sure seems like you do, *Alex.*"

I clench my jaw, anger brewing in my veins at her insinuation. Before Jana, I hadn't kissed anyone since Laura died.

"As fun as it is to watch you ream him," Benji interrupts, shooting a smirk in my direction, "he hasn't so much as *thought* of another woman since Laura passed. Believe me, I've tried setting him up more times than I can count. But Jana...well, he hasn't been able to shut up about her."

"He still kissed Leslie," Wren reminds him softly.

"Yeah, but Leslie's crazy," Benji replies, shrugging. "She's always been batshit about Alex, but we never thought anything would come of it, since, you know, he married her sister."

"Leslie's been through a lot," I say in her defense, but I regret it almost immediately.

"So has Jana." Hadlee's voice is cold and sharp. "She's been cheated on so many times, she doesn't know how to trust anyone anymore. We finally got her to let her guard down, to open herself up to love again, and you fucked it up"

No wonder she's so hurt.

"Hadlee, I didn't cheat on her."

"Sure looks like you did."

If I didn't already feel like an idiot, I do now. Jana's heart was vulnerable, and I didn't guard it the way I was supposed to. The need to fix this grows tenfold, knowing this simple misunderstanding is a full-blown betrayal in her eyes.

"I need your help—"

"I already told you, Alex," Wren says, shaking her head. "We're on her side."

"I have a plan to fix it all," I say. "But I can't pull it off by myself."

The girls look at each other, doubts flickering in the depths of Wren's eyes.

"How do we know you're not just gonna fuck it up again?" Hadlee asks.

"You don't," I say with a sigh. "But I'd like the chance to prove I won't."

"Alex—" Hadlee shakes her head, but I cut her off.

"I love her, Hadlee." I say. "I love her with every piece of my heart. She *is* my heart. I've already let too much time pass without telling her that, and I don't want to wait any longer. I need her—I can't go the rest of my life without her by my side. I just can't."

"*Damn.*" Benji and Wren's voices merge in a soft whisper.

"How are you thinking you'll fix this?" Hadlee asks, leaning her hip on the table beside her. She still looks skeptical, but I think I've brought Wren around.

"A grand gesture." I reply, smiling for the first time today.

"What is that supposed to mean?"

"Just…" I shake my head, a laugh slipping out. Relief floods through me, knowing I've got a chance. "Can you get her to the bookshop Thursday night?"

"Won't the booths be set up by then?" Wren asks, leaning forward in her chair. "The festival starts on Friday."

"Yes," I say, grinning. "And ours will be set up in front of the bookshop."

"What are you gonna do?" Hadlee asks again.

"Don't worry about it, Hadlee," I say. "Your only job is to get Jana in front of the bookstore just after sundown. Benji, Wren, and I will handle the rest."

CHAPTER TWENTY-THREE
JANA

Exhaling slowly, I blow out the pain that's been lingering in my heart for the last few days. After his last attempt to talk to me at the bakery, Alex hasn't tried to see me. I miss him, more than I want to admit. A part of me hates that he gave up so easily, especially after he vowed to make things right.

"How does it look?" Quinn calls from the other side of the door. I blink out of my thoughts and shake my head before focusing on my reflection in the mirror. The dress she picked out leaves little to the imagination, hugging all my curves in just the right way. I flip my unruly curls to the side, admiring the way the deep red fabric of the dress looks against my pale skin. "Come on, we want to see it!"

I open the bathroom door and step out with a hesitant smile. "I don't know, guys...I don't really want to go out tonight."

"HAWTIE!" Quinn squeals, ignoring my desperate attempt to get out of this girls night out. "Damn, look at you! Who knew you had such a hot bod under all those sweaters?"

"Shut up." I roll my eyes as a flush creeps up my neck.

"She's right though, Jay," Hadlee says from her spot on the bed. "You look *good*."

I cross my arms, feeling a little uncomfortable under their scrutinizing gazes. It's been a long time since I went out in something so tight, and my anxiety flares to life as Quinn approaches me. I bite the inside of my cheek, waiting for her calculating gaze to stop analyzing me.

"Red lipstick," she says.

"Seriously, I don't think I should go," I say, tapping nervously on my forearm. Leaving the house feels impossible normally, but now? In this dress?

"You've got to get out of this house before you go insane," Hadlee says, holding up a tube of lipstick. Quinn takes it and gestures for me to pucker my lips. "You're driving me crazy, and I'm not even getting treats out of it this time."

I blush as Quinn smears the lipstick over my lips. It's true; baking has become a rarity around the house. Instead, I lay around reading or watching movies to keep my mind occupied. Baking offers too much thinking time, and those thoughts make me cry more.

"I just...I don't want to even *chance* a run-in with him," I admit. Sitting on the edge of my bed, I tug on wool-lined tights and a pair of cute black booties. "It just hurts too much."

"That's why we're going to a club in Bozeman," Quinn says, checking her reflection in the mirror. She straightened her hair and pulled it up into a sleek ponytail. Her makeup is dramatic, with a dark smokey eye and a bright red lip. Her black dress is much shorter than mine, making her legs look even longer than normal. The heeled booties complete the look, giving her an extra four inches. "There's no chance he'll be there."

"We're going out, and you're coming with us," Hadlee says, standing up. She adjusts her dress, pulling her boobs back up into position. It's a gorgeous shade of red, slightly darker than mine, with long sleeves and a deep V that shoots down between her breasts. The hemline is short like Quinn's, accentuating her already long legs. Her heels are strappy gold sandals, which match her hoop earrings and the long chains around her neck. She looks at me, her green eyes accentuated by heavy black lashes. "Tonight's about you, Jay. I promise you're going to love it."

I shoot my friends a confused glance when Hadlee pulls over on the far end of Main Street and turns off the engine.

"Come on," she says, opening the door.

"This isn't Bozeman," Quinn points out but follows her anyway.

"It got her out of the house, didn't it?" Hadlee shoots back, rolling her eyes.

I glance out the window, my heart skittering. The sun is just beginning to sink behind the mountains, but that doesn't deter the residents of Harmony. Twinkling lights line the street, keeping it lit bright as day. *Alex could be out there.*

"I think I'll stay here."

"Don't be a party pooper, Jan," Quinn says, pulling open my door. "Wren is waiting for us up the street a bit. Come on."

"I don't know..."

"Would you just get out of the damn car?" Hadlee grouches, her heels clicking against the icy road. She bounces in place, trying to keep herself warm. I bite my lip, nerves flooding through me as I climb out of the car. The temperature has begun to drop as the sun sinks lower, and I tug my coat tightly around my body.

With Harmony's Christmas festival starting tomorrow, the street is lined with booths, waiting to be filled with goodies. The girls each link arms with me, tugging me toward the center of all the booths.

"This is a bad idea," I say as we get closer to Brooks Books. I can see the storefront from here, still dark next to the rest of the brightly lit stores. *I never did convince him to decorate.* "I don't think I can do this."

"I promise, it'll be worth it, Jay," Hadlee whispers in my ear. Her fingers lace with mine, and she gives my hand a soft squeeze. I suck in a deep breath, the cold air burning my lungs. I allow my friends to lead me further down the street, closer to the bookshop, and my eyes catch on the only booth that's set up.

"What..." I blink in surprise, my mouth falling open.

Twinkle lights weave through the garland wrapped around the poles of the tent. A slender bookshelf stands to the side, lights draped around each shelf, holding delicately wrapped books. A small table sits beside it, draped in a holly-covered tablecloth and waiting for the bakery items. The giant prize wheel is set up next to the table, and a tree takes up the back corner of the booth, prizes hanging from it like ornaments.

It's absolutely perfect.

The girls let go of me, and I move forward, my fingers tracing over the shelves. "When did..."

A flash of lights catches me off guard, and I lift my gaze to the bookstore behind the booths. Tears spring to my eyes at the sight before me. Maddie and Morgan sprint from the front door, their giggles filling the night air.

"Miss Jana!"

"Do you like it? Daddy said you would love it!"

"I missed you, Miss Jana!"

I'm overwhelmed by the emotions that rush through me as the girls race into my arms. My heart warms as they wrap their little arms around me. Losing them was one of the hardest parts of this whole situation. I truly love these little girls more than anything, and having them back in my arms makes everything fall away.

"I missed you girls so much," I say, my voice catching on tears. I blink through the tears and hold them at arm's length. "Did you help your daddy with that?"

I gesture to the bookshop, and the girls nod enthusiastically. They each grab a hand and tug at me until I follow them around the booth. We stand on the sidewalk, staring up at the storefront. Gone is the macabre display. Bright lights frame the bookstore window, bringing attention to a new display. A tree stands to one side, books perched on the branches. An overstuffed armchair sits beside it, the new home of Maddie's old teddy bears, who each hold a book.

The final touch is big bold lettering painted across the window reading *"Merry Christmas, Jana!"*

"What do you think, darling?" Alex asks from behind me, his breath warm on my neck. My vision blurs as I turn to face him, his heady cologne enveloping me like a warm hug. The girls drop my hands and run to where Wren, Benji, Quinn, and Hadlee wait, leaving me to face Alex on my own.

"It's beautiful," I say, my voice a broken whisper. I blink quickly, trying to clear my vision of tears before he notices them, but I'm already too late. His hand is there, at my cheek, before I can say anything more, his thumb trailing through the tear track.

"*You're* beautiful." His voice is gravelly, and I catch my breath. His fingers trail up, catching in my curls, and he leans in, resting his forehead against mine. "*God*, I've missed you, Jana."

I missed you, too.

The image of him kissing Leslie flares to life, and I step back, shaking my head. My heart is beating a mile a minute, more tears collecting on my waterline. "I-I can't do this."

My words are breathless, and as I stumble back, Alex catches my hand in his. "Please let me explain. The kiss you saw meant nothing."

I breathe out a laugh, shocked by his nonchalance. "*Every* kiss means something, Alex."

"No, they don't," he says firmly, pulling me closer. The tears fall, a sob building in my chest. His hand cups my cheek again, and he forces me to look up at him. Our eyes lock, and I'm lost in depths of amber and gold. "*Our* kisses mean everything—*you* mean *everything*."

My heart jumps at his admission.

"I want to believe that," I say, hating how vulnerable I feel right now. "But I saw you—"

"I know what you saw, Jana, but I pulled away." He pauses, caressing my cheek as he leans closer. Our lips are only a breath apart, and my stomach clenches in anticipation. The world feels like it's moving in slow motion as he smiles softly. "Because there's only one woman in this world I want to hold."

He wraps his arm around my waist, pulling me tight against his chest.

"To kiss."

His lips brush mine in the lightest touch, and my eyes flutter.

"*To love.*"

My heart skips, and tears slide freely down my cheeks. Alex closes the distance between us, claiming my lips in a slow, languid kiss. He's warm and gentle, holding me like I'll break. Something tells me everything he said is true, and I let go of the doubt that tries to cling to my heart. I relax in his hold and melt into the kiss. I've never felt this way about someone before, and knowing Alex feels the same way sets my heart on fire.

CHAPTER TWENTY-FOUR
JANA

Finding love in my hometown of Harmony, Montana was never my intention, but even the best laid plans can go awry. Standing on Main Street amidst the two dozen booths, fresh snow coating each tent and lamppost, it feels almost surreal.

My eyes track Maddie and Morgan through the winding track they take, chasing after their uncle Benji. Their joy warms my heart, and now I know what it is to have people to live for. They pause in front of a booth across the way, eyes lighting up at the sight of the cotton candy. I laugh as they beg Benji to get them some before dragging him toward the pony rides.

The laughter that rings through the festival makes my heart swell, even though the chilly winter air tries to dampen our moods. Alex wraps his arms around my waist, resting his chin on my shoulder, and overwhelming *rightness* fills me. *I'm exactly where I'm supposed to be.*

"Well, booth buddy," Alex whispers in my ear, making me chuckle. I haven't used the term since the beginning of this partnership, yet he brings it back like an inside joke. And I suppose it is. "We did it."

"What exactly did we do, *booth buddy*?"

"Well, for one," he starts, pressing a light kiss to my neck. Butterflies erupt at his feather-like touches, a shiver racing down my spine. "We made it to the festival without killing each other."

"That's true." I grin, leaning into his embrace.

"And…" His breath is hot on my chilled skin, and I squirm against him. "We sold out of 'Blind Date with a Book' on day one."

"We did?" I jerk away from him in surprise, and he drops his arms from my waist with a deep chuckle. I glance at the shelves, surprised to see them all empty. Excitement floods through me, and I turn to face him. "Alex, do you know what this means?"

"What?"

"People love the 'Blind Date with a Book' idea!" I explain, ideas racing through my head. "What if you made it a permanent display in the shop?"

"You think it'll drive more sales?" he asks, gripping my hips to pull me closer. I rest my hands on his arms, smiling up at him.

"It might, yeah."

"Well then, I think it's a brilliant idea, darling." He grins down at me, nudging my nose with his. He leans down further, pressing his mouth to mine in a heated kiss. Heat races down my spine, erasing all thought from my mind as he traces his tongue over my lips. My lips part, and he takes the opportunity to deepen the kiss. Everything falls away, leaving only Alex and me, wrapped together in the heat of our kiss.

When he pulls away, I stare up at him in a daze. His grin is devilish, his eyes a darker shade of amber than before. He pushes loose curls behind my ear then swipes his thumb over my bottom lip. "Now, do you want to keep people watching, darling?"

I nod, speechless. He chuckles, pressing a kiss to my forehead. He shaved this morning, so the skin is stubbly, scratching gently against my face. He turns me around, pulling my back into his chest. I sink into his embrace, feeling perfectly at home in his arms. I smile to myself, leaning my head against his shoulder.

"So..." I look up at him. "What are we going to do for the rest of the weekend now that the 'Blind Dates' are sold out?"

"I'm sure we can find some more books somewhere," he jokes, nuzzling his face into the crook of my neck. I giggle as his stubble tickles the sensitive flesh there, and feel his lips turn up in a smile. "How do you want to celebrate, darling?"

"Celebrate?"

"That's right."

"And what are we celebrating, booth buddy?" I ask, raising an eyebrow. He chuckles at the nickname, nipping lightly at the juncture of my neck. I catch my breath, tensing in his arms. "Surely not the extra work we've made for ourselves."

"How about..." His breath is hot on my neck as he presses soft, open-mouthed kisses to my neck. "The fact that the woman I love...is in love with me?"

"Hmmm," I moan softly, feeling a smile tug at my lips. "That *is* something to celebrate, isn't it?"

His lips trail up my neck until they caress my ear. A shiver shoots down my spine, and I bite my bottom lip to keep from shifting away. "You bet that pretty little ass it's something to celebrate, darling."

EPILOGUE
ALEX

Opening the front door, I let Jana step through before following her. The house is quiet and dark, a stark contrast to the usual state of my home. The Christmas tree gives off a soft glow, and as we walk further into the house, I feel a sense of peace wash over me.

"It was nice of Benji to take the girls tonight," Jana says softly, turning to face me. Seeing her here, in my home, sends a spark through me. Her dark curls have an ethereal glow from the twinkle lights, and her eyes hold a glint of mischief.

"He knew I wanted to have some time with you all to myself," I say, stepping into her space. She smiles shyly up at me, her cheeks tinged a soft pink. I pull her into my arms, loving the way her curves fit perfectly against me. The scent of her honey and cinnamon shampoo wraps around me, and I press my face into her hair to get my fill. "*God*, you have no idea how much I've missed you, darling."

"I missed you, too, Alex." Her voice is barely above a whisper as it slides over me.

"You've wormed your way into every part of my life, Jana," I say, trying to make it clear to her just how much I need her. She tilts her head back, her big brown eyes finding mine in the dim light. She looks like an angel, and my arms instinctively tighten around her. "You're everything to me; I can't function without you."

"What do you mean?" she asks. Her lips—*God, those lips*—turn up in a half smile, curiosity filling her face. I look away for half a second, embarrassment flooding through me. Her laugh brings my gaze back to her, to that mouth—*God, that mouth*. "Are you blushing?"

I shake my head, laughing lightly. "I tried to make cookies..."

Jana raises her eyebrows.

"And I burned them."

Her bright laugh fills the house, and I grin at the sound. *I could get used to this.*

"What kind?"

"What?"

"What kind of cookies did you try to make?" She waits expectantly for my answer.

"Oatmeal chocolate chip." They're my favorite, and it was a recipe I've used before, yet somehow, they turned out horribly wrong.

"Well," she says, smiling mischievously. She takes my hand in hers, leading me further inside. "Why don't we make some together?"

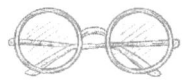

What we make is a big mess.

Jana grins at me, her dimples on full display as she sets the kitchen timer. "You'd better go find the broom, Mr. Hall."

"Don't worry, darling," I say, backing her up against the counter. Our clothes are covered in flour, and if the light dusting in her hair is anything to go on, I'm sure we'll both need a shower. "I'll get this all cleaned up in no time."

My hands find her hips and squeeze gently before making their way down to the backs of her thighs. Her soft gasp is enough to make me groan. Her thighs dimple beneath my fingers, and she lets out a cute little squeal as I lift her carefully onto the counter. Her leggings will be covered in flour, but at this point, I can't care. I part her legs, inserting myself between them and pulling her firmly against me.

"What are you doing?" she asks, breathless.

"Kissing you, if that's alright?" I reply. That smile is back, and she nods, leaning in to meet me. She lifts her hands to my cheeks, trailing up into my hair as she looks deeply into my eyes.

Our breath mingles, and I keep my hands firmly on her hips, waiting for her.

She leans closer; our noses bump, lips brushing lightly.

"I love you, Alex," she sighs against my lips.

My grip tightens, and I press my mouth firmly against hers. Every time our lips connect, I'm left breathless and wanting more. I groan into her mouth, a full-body shiver working its way from my head to my toes. I'll never get enough of Jana or her soft lips.

It's a slow, leisurely kiss, our lips brushing together softly. I let her lead, enjoying the combination of her fingernails against my scalp and her gentle kiss. Her tongue brushes mine softly, and I fight the urge to deepen the kiss—to take everything she has to offer.

She pulls away a moment later, resting her forehead against mine. Her eyes are still closed, and I smile at the sight. She exhales slowly, her lashes fluttering open. Her pupils are dilated, almost the entire starburst of gold enveloped. I love seeing how I affect her, knowing she affects me in the same way.

"I love you, Jana." Her breath catches, and I press another soft kiss to her lips. "You are beautiful, inside and out. I'm the luckiest man in the world because I get to love you."

"Forever and always?"

"Forever and always, darling."

ACKNOWLEDGMENTS

I could spend a lifetime putting my heart and soul into words on paper, but it would never amount to anything without the people in my life who have supported me through thick and thin. This story would never have reached its full potential without the wonderful team of people behind me.

To my husband: Aus, it's you and me against the world. Thank you for being my rock, my shoulder to cry on, my eternal companion in this life and the next. I never would've made this leap without your support and love. Thank you for the late-night talks, helping me through plot holes and other stresses. Thank you for getting up early with the boys so I could get an extra hour of sleep. Thank you for being you, for being a better man and husband than I ever could've asked for. I appreciate you beyond words, and I don't think I'll ever believe that I deserve your immense love.

To Keri: Thank you for being such an amazing friend and PA. You are a blessing in my life, and I will never stop singing your praises. Thank you for the late-night voice memos and the constant cheerleading. I never would've found the courage to rewrite this story without your encouragement, but I'm so glad we did! Alex and Jana received the story they deserve because of you, and I love you so much for it.

To Tori Lewis: You've been an incredible friend, and I'm beyond grateful for your support and love through this crazy writing process. You inspire me every day, and I wouldn't be where I am without you. Thank you for being so authentically you, and for encouraging me to be unapologetically me. I love you.

To my Alpha Readers: Taylor, Kara, and Tiffany. Thank you so much! The support you have shown since you've joined my team has been incredible, and I am blown away. You've been a light in the dark through this whole process, and I truly believe you are one of the only reasons this story has found its way into the daylight. I never would've made it here without your love and excitement for this book. Thank you; I love you.

To my boys: James, Theo, and Little Bear. You have been my biggest cheerleaders through this whole journey, and I can only hope that excitement continues through the years. There is nothing I would love more than to teach you to chase your dreams, even when they feel impossible—*especially* when they feel impossible. Never give up, my darlings—you'll never know how far you can go if you do. I love you, forever and always.

And finally, to God. Thank You for giving me this dream and the desire to reach it. Thank You for sending these wonderful people into my life at just the right time—You always know exactly what and who I need, and for that I will always be grateful. Lord, I thank You for the trials you've put in my path so that I could become who I am now. None of this would've been possible without You and Your love. Thank You, Lord. I love you.

ABOUT THE AUTHOR

Kalayna Marie lives in Northern Utah with her extremely supportive husband and two, almost three, sons. She's been writing full-time since fall of 2022, with no plans to stop anytime soon. Her debut series, Love in Harmony, is set to have 5 novels in total with the first releasing this November. When she's not writing you can usually find her reading, playing with her boys, or playing Scrabble with her husband.